SWEET ENTANGLEMENT

INDIGO BAY SWEET ROMANCE

JEAN C. GORDON

Upstate NY Romance

ISBN-13: 978-1-7321836-0-5

Sweet Entanglement

Cover art by Najla Qamber Designs

Much thanks to my critique group, BFF
(Bonnie, Colleen, Chris, and Thomasine),
my editor Jena O'Connor,
my cover designer, Najla Qamber,
and last but not least, the Sweet Reads author group
for inviting me to visit Indigo Bay with them.
I couldn't have done it without you.

INDIGO BAY SWEET ROMANCE

What is the Indigo Bay Sweet Romance Series? It's tons of fun for readers! But more specifically, it's a set of books written by authors who love romance. Grab a glass of sweet tea, sit on the porch, and get ready to be swept away into this charming South Carolina Beach town.

The Indigo Bay world has been written so readers can dive in anywhere in the series without missing a beat. Read one or all—they're all sweet, fun rides that you won't soon forget. Also as special treats, you'll see some recurring characters. How many can you find?

Sweet Saturday by Pamela Kelley

Sweet Beginnings by Melissa McClone

Sweet Starlight by Kay Correll

Sweet Forgiveness by Jean Oram

Sweet Reunion by Stacy Claflin

Sweet Entanglement by Jean C. Gordon

Jean C. Gordon's writing is a natural extension of her love of reading. From that day in first grade when she realized t-h-e was the word the, she's been reading everything she can put her hands on. Jean and her college-sweetheart husband share a 175-year-old farmhouse in Upstate New York with their daughter and her family. Their son lives nearby.

Connect with Jean on Facebook, facebook.com/jeancgordon.author, as @JeanCGordon on Twitter, or on JeanCGordon.com. And make sure you don't miss any of my releases, promotions, and giveaways, by signing up for my Readers Group newsletter at http://bit.ly/JCGReaders.

BOOKS BY JEAN C. GORDON
THE NO BRIDES CLUB

Six friends make a pact not to let love get in the way of their careers, and the No Brides Club is born. But could meeting the right man at the wrong time cause them to break their vows to each other?

No Time for Apologies (Book 5)

TEAM MACACHEK

Fall in love with the strong women and fearless men of the motocross circuit

Mending the Motocross Champion
(Meet teenage Jesse and Lauren)
Holiday Escape
A Team Macachek Christmas
(Prequel to Sweet Entanglement)

UPSTATE NY . . . WHERE LOVE IS
A LITTLE SWEETER

Bachelor Father
Love Undercover
Mandy and the Mayor
Candy Kisses
Mara's Move

LOVE INSPIRED
BRIDGES

Reuniting His Family
A Mom for His Daughter

THE DONNELLY BROTHERS

Hometown boys make good…and find love

Winning the Teacher's Heart
Holiday Homecoming
The Bachelor's Sweetheart

SMALL-TOWN

Small-Town Sweethearts
Small-Town Mom
Small-Town Dad
Small-Town Midwife

ANTHOLOGY—THE
MATCHMAKERS

A Match Made in Williamstown

CHAPTER 1

Jesse Brewster ran his tongue around the inside of his mouth and tried to swallow the grit. He didn't know if it was actual sand from the South Carolina beach he tried to sleep on last night or the tequila shots he'd downed like water after he'd gotten a good look at the monstrosity that was supposed to be his life-saving legacy.

"Sir, your public defender is here," a male voice said.

Jesse opened his eyes to the neon yellow walls surrounding him, reflecting back every sharp ray of light from the inside lighting and small window. He squinted against the pain to his head. Someone here at the Indigo Bay, South Carolina, police department had some sense of humor painting the combination interrogation room/holding cell walls bright yellow with royal blue trim. The sleeping block and covers he was sitting on and the table and chairs were the same blue.

"Thanks." Jesse squinted again at the police officer's name badge. "Officer Andrews." The man looked vaguely familiar. Probably his arresting officer.

That would make sense, him being here for his arraignment.

"The dispatcher will bring you some breakfast. You can eat while you talk with your lawyer. The judge will be over as soon as she finishes her coffee at Caroline's."

"Coffee will be fine," Jesse said. He closed his eyes against the yellow and held his head in his palms.

A minute later footsteps sounded. "Sir."

What was with all this sir? Jesse shook his head to clear it. The bright paint hadn't just affected his sight. His ears were also hallucinating.

"I'm Lauren Cooper, the public defender."

He raised his head. No, his ears were right. It was Lauren.

"Jesse?"

Her voice dripped with disbelief that matched his own. And he'd thought things couldn't get any worse. "In the flesh." He flexed his bicep, unable to resist going full obnoxious, in case she still harbored any positive thoughts about who, what he was.

"You didn't have any ID on you, and apparently declined to identify yourself to the officer."

By reflex, Jesse patted the back pocket of his jeans. No wallet. A vague picture of it on a bar swam before his eyes.

Lauren dropped the folder she'd held to the table and pulled out one of the chairs, giving him a moment to study her. He raked his hand though his matted hair. She looked good. But when didn't Lauren look good? Her crisp power suit did nothing to hinder his memories of the soft curves beneath them. His stomach churned with something that had nothing to do with his excess of tequila.

She motioned to the other chair. "If you'd care to join me, I'll go over the charges. Ben … Officer Andrews said you may not have had the capacity to understand them last night."

Ben, was it? Jesse's gaze darted from Lauren to the hallway the officer had disappeared into. He stood, letting the spinning in his head stop before he took the two steps from the sleeping block to the table. What did he care? He and Lauren were over. He'd made sure of that. They'd been growing apart, going in different directions. He didn't need to get into the direction he'd been headed after his accident and his mother's death—with himself or anyone else. Jesse looked around. He'd arrived at his destination. There was nowhere to go now, but up.

"Any questions?" Lauren pinned his gaze with hers. "Let me rephrase that. Did you listen to a word I said?"

"Public intoxication. Vagrancy. How'd I do?"

Officer Andrews appeared at the door. "Lauren, the judge is here."

She rose. "We're ready."

He didn't get a say? Jesse wasn't sure he liked this take-charge Lauren. But wasn't that one of the reasons he'd let her go? So, she could reach her potential, as his mom might have said. His throat clogged with the loss that would always be too fresh.

"Before we go into the court room, I have an ID for your vagrant. Jesse Brewster and I are old friends." She handed the officer a sheet from her folder.

So, they were still friends. Some of the darkness in Jess's soul lifted, not that meant much. There was plenty left. He gauged the other man's reaction. Aside from a raised brow, he didn't have any outward reaction to Lauren's statement.

"Brewster," the man said, offering his hand.

Jesse wiped his gritty palm against the pant-leg of his jeans. "Under different circumstances, I'd say nice to meet you." He forced a smile.

"Brewster," the officer repeated. "You used to race. Motocross."

"Yes, yes, I did," Jesse said tightly, bracing for the judgmental look from the officer and Lauren.

"We shouldn't keep Judge Trexler waiting," Lauren said.

If she'd interrupted for his benefit, because of their friendship, she shouldn't have bothered. He knew what he'd done, who he was now far better than she did, and he was a big boy, ready to move past it.

They walked upstairs to the city hall adjoining the police department and into a large room with rows of chairs facing the court bench. A middle-aged woman sat behind it with another woman seated to her right and a man in a suit standing in front of the bench talking to them.

"Judge Trexler, the court clerk, and the city attorney," Lauren explained as they entered the room.

Officer Andrews led Jesse to the front row, where the three of them took their seats, Lauren on one side of him and the officer on the other. The city attorney sat next to officer Andrews.

The judge called the court into session. "Mr. Johnson and Ms. Cooper, please approach the bench."

Jesse shifted in his chair as bits of the conversation drifted back to him. "Identified. No damage. Vagrancy. Vouch."

"Mr. Brewster."

The judge's voice jerked Jesse's gaze from where it rested on Lauren's back.

"Please join us."

Officer Andrews walked him the few feet to the bench, as if he were going to make a break for it.

"Your Honor." Jesse nodded in respect.

"The city attorney has agreed to drop the vagrancy charges since your wallet with ID has been found and turned into the court and to reduce the other charge to sleeping on the beach, a violation with a fine. How do you plead to the charge? You can consult with your attorney."

"Guilty." He had several things he'd like to consult with Lauren about, but his sleeping on the beach wasn't one.

"Your plea is accepted. You can settle the fine with my clerk. Any questions?"

"No, but I want to clarify that I definitely am not a vagrant, and further, I'm not a tourist. I'm Indigo Bay's newest property-owner."

$\sim$

The slightly wide-eyed surprise that accompanied Judge Trexler's "Welcome to Indigo Bay" after Jesse had dropped his bombshell didn't come within a thousand miles of the surprise and other jumble of feelings careening through Lauren. She breathed in until her lungs were close to bursting to compose herself.

"Thank you. It looks like a fine community," Jesse said, nodding to the judge before he turned his attention to her.

"Thank you, Judge," Lauren repeated. She lifted her hand to touch Jesse's arm and dropped it. "This way, Mr. Brewster."

"Mr. Brewster, is it?" he said in a low, just-for-her voice as he stepped beside her moving toward the court clerk.

She flushed, a curse of her fair hair and skin. "For now," she ground out between her teeth. "We need to talk when you're done here."

He favored her with a slow smile before he stepped up to the clerk behind the bench. The smile she'd once thought of as her smile. Her chest hollowed. He probably used it with all his women.

"First, here's your wallet," the clerk said. "The bar owner turned it in this morning. Check to make sure everything is there."

Jesse took the wallet and shoved it in his back pocket. "I'm sure it is."

Lauren bit her tongue to stop herself from telling Jesse to check his wallet. Indigo Bay was a small, close-knit community, but it also was a tourist spot and had its share of petty crime.

"I have some forms for you to sign." The clerk pushed a couple of papers toward Jesse. "And your fine will be three hundred and fifty dollars. We take cash, certified check or money order, or a major credit card."

Lauren waited a step back for Jesse to whip his wallet back out and plunk the cash or, more likely a credit card, on the wooden bench top. The Jesse she knew, generally didn't carry large amounts of cash with him when it could be deposited somewhere to make more money.

Jesse cleared his throat. "When does it have to be paid?"

"Within thirty days."

"Are there any other options? I'm not in a … let's say a good financial position."

Jesse's rigid stance told Lauren what it took out of him to make that admission.

"Judge," the clerk said. "Could you step over here?"

While Judge Trexler finished her conversation with Ben and the city attorney and made her way over, Lauren stared at the back of the man she'd once known so well, the man she didn't know at all anymore. *Her* Jesse, wouldn't have been in a financial bind. He'd have had every extra cent he had invested for emergencies and the future. She swallowed hard. For their future. So he could retire from motocross in his late twenties or early thirties and be set. To blow through that kind of money, he must have gone even crazier after his accident than the motocross fan magazines had reported. Lauren's gaze traveled down his dirty, weathered, form-fitting jeans for any sign of the injury that cut his career short, but she didn't see one.

"Are you willing to do community service?" Judge Trexler asked.

Lauren had been so intent on Jesse, she hadn't noticed the judge join the clerk and Jesse.

"Yes, ma'am."

"Since you'll be on the beach anyway …"

On the beach? Lauren shook her head to clear it. What had she missed? Jesse was the only person who could ever knock her off focus.

"… The city attorney said they're short a person on the public beach clean-up crew. One of the college students got a better job. Work starts at sun-up and finishes at eight when the beach opens. Four weeks at half pay will work off your fine."

"Sounds good to me, and thanks again."

Lauren snapped shut her dropped-open jaw. International racing phenom Jesse Brewster picking up trash?

The judge motioned to her clerk. "Annie will get you set up."

Once the judge had left, Lauren touched Jesse's shoulder, rethinking her earlier statement about talking with Jesse. "I need to get back to the office."

"We'll only be two minutes," Annie said. "Then you and your friend Mr. Brewster …"

"Jesse," he interrupted.

"You and Jesse can go have a coffee and something sweet at Caroline's.

Her friend? Where had Annie gotten that from? Ben was the only one she'd told that she knew Jesse, and Ben had been with them. She bit and released her lip. It didn't matter, and it wasn't like she was going to hide that she knew Jesse. "I really should get back to work," she said. And look up what property Jesse owned in Indigo Bay, along with anything else recent she could find on him. She needed to be prepared to talk with him.

"Acer and Acer won't miss you if you take an hour to catch up with your friend," Annie said. "What are the guys doing this morning anyway? Reading *The Wall Street Journal* and the *Charleston Post and Courierr*, as usual?

Probably. But having coffee with Jesse wouldn't generate billable hours. Besides, the partners didn't like her spending too much time on her fill-in public defender work. Expanding their contract with the city as back-up counsel to also provide services when the public defender's office was swamped had been her idea to fill some of her down time. Even though it brought steady income to the firm, the work didn't generate the fees real estate and estate work did. And if she weren't there, who would be doing the research grunt work for the real estate and estate business, which Lauren admitted she did willingly. She'd joined Acer and Acer because it was the largest law firm in town revenue-wise, and the retirement-age owners had offered her a fast track to partner.

Lauren glanced at Jesse's stony expression. He didn't look any more anxious to get together with her than she was with him. Perversity took over. "You're right. An hour won't hurt."

∾

Jesse scratched his signature on the form the clerk had slid across the bench to him. This wasn't the way he'd planned on reconnecting with Lauren. Not that he had plans for reconnecting. *No.* Who was he kidding. He'd thought about seeing her at one of the Christmas galas Team Macachek threw every year for current and former members and employees of the team. But that picture had him attending as a successful business owner, not the down-on-his-luck man he was at the moment.

He pasted on a smile and faced Lauren. "So, what's this Caroline's everyone keeps talking about?"

She drew her lips into a smile that looked as fake as his must look to her. "Sweet Caroline's Café. Just the best coffee and selection of sweets in Indigo Bay."

And most likely a gathering place for the good citizens of Indigo Bay. He and Lauren stepped out into the hot bright mid-morning sun, and his stomach grumbled with hunger, he hoped, and not in protest of last night. He glanced down at his grimy t-shirt.

"It's a couple blocks. Do you want to walk? I could drive," Lauren said.

His back itched between his shoulder blades, where he knew he couldn't reach. "How far is the beach?"

Lauren knitted her brows and laughed. "The beach is never far in Indigo Bay. Why?"

"What I'd really like is to go back to the beach and grab my truck." He patted the front pocket of his jeans, and to his relief felt his keys. "Then go clean up."

She eyed him, sending the itch down his spine.

"No coffee first? I could run in and get you a large, black, with one of Caroline's famous cinnamon rolls."

"Famous, huh," he quipped to hide the tick in his heart rate caused by her remembering how he took his coffee. Then why wouldn't she? They'd known each other for ten years, since they were seventeen, when he'd thought black coffee was macho. The taste for it came later.

"Rated number one in *The Observer's* food and drink reviews."

"I'm sold, but maybe we should walk." He rubbed his hands down the front of his jeans, and they came off gritty. "I don't want to get your car all dirty."

"Not a problem. I have a black lab/shepherd mix who likes to ride shotgun. It would be another story if you wanted to drive my car, sit in my seat."

His gaze dropped to the side and down to her behind at the thought of her settling in behind the wheel. Warm appreciation replaced his nanosecond of disgust. *Hey.* He was a guy.

Lauren led him to a green crossover SUV in the Indigo Bay City Hall parking lot. He let himself in the passenger side, while she got behind the wheel and turned the vehicle on. In a minute, they reached their destination.

With a sudden jerk of the steering wheel, Lauren pulled into a parking space hot on the tailgate of the truck pulling out. "It doesn't look too busy. I'll be back in two minutes." She was out of the car before he could pull his wallet out of his pocket. For all the good it would have done. He wasn't sure he had enough cash on him to pay for a coffee and cinnamon roll. While he waited, Jesse checked out Seaside Boulevard, starting with the bright blue awning of Sweet Caroline's Café. It looked like other small-town beach communities he'd been to on the racing circuit, except a little cleaner, more cheerful, and prosperous than many.

Lauren returned a few minutes later. "Here you go. My treat."

"Thanks." Jesse took the food and drink, avoiding eye contact

She pulled out onto the boulevard. A few moments of silence hung between them before she asked, "You do know where your truck is?"

"I sure do. It has my bike trailer attached." His one and only motorcycle, a come down from the three he'd once owned.

Her lips twitched, and he unconsciously turned his head and leaned toward her before he stopped himself by dusting a dog hair off the dashboard. "Dog hair. The Old Morrison Place."

She stared at him.

"My truck. It's parked there. At the end of Sandy Lane, off Beachside Boulevard." In their correspondence, Mr. Acer had called the property the Old Morrison place as if that was how the locals knew it.

"I know where it is. That's private property."

Lauren didn't know? She worked for the law firm that had settled his great-uncle Jim Morrison's estate.

"We'd better get over there before you're cited again. This time for trespassing."

His stomach knotted. That's what Lauren thought of him? A criminal nuisance? Considering her profession and their reunion, he shouldn't be surprised. "It's not a problem. I know the owner."

Lauren hit the brakes harder than necessary at one of the few traffic lights, he'd noticed in town. "You do?" Her voice pitched louder in question. "Mr. Morrison died a couple of years ago. People have been speculating about the new owner since. Some distant relative, but as far as I know, no new deed has been registered with the county."

"His grand-nephew," Jesse said.

"Someone you know from racing?"

"You might say that." He was enjoying keeping Lauren on tenterhooks, if only for the attractive flush it brought to her cheeks that reminded him of the girl he'd once known.

Lauren slowed to a stop at the end of Sandy Lane next to the house and a few feet from his truck. "Come on, tell me."

"You're looking at him."

She glanced past Jesse and out the window.

"Me-ee." Jesse drew the word out.

"You? For real?" Lauren threw open the door and hopped out of the car. "I've been dying to see the inside the house since I moved here. It's the last of the original beach mansions left standing."

Jesse looked at the structure's missing and drooping shutters and the decided tilt of one corner of the house. "The still-standing may only be a matter of time. The city is on the verge of condemning the property."

Lauren nodded. "Sad. Mom's been here about five years, and Mr. Morrison had already been in a nursing home for a quite a while before that. Alzheimers. His brother didn't want to sell the property, but he didn't maintain it, either." She shrugged. "And I don't know how well Mr. Morrison was able to take care of it before he went in the home. Both brothers died within weeks of each other. No children or grandchildren."

"And so it came to me." A sand crab scuttled past the toe of his boot. "Mr. Morrison was my mother's uncle."

"You just found out about the house, your inheritance?"

He dug his toe into the crab's path. "No, I've known for a while. The lawyers finally got it all worked out six months or so ago." Jesse eyed Lauren for a reaction.

"And you didn't bother to come until now?"

There it was. The question. The Lauren he remembered always had questions, wanted to know details. That was her nature, especially after her parents' marriage had broken up and her father had left without her having an inkling it was coming. And, with the question came the bar he could never measure up to. *Not good enough, Brewster.*

"Under the circumstances, I didn't think it was important."

Lauren blanched. "Your mother. I'm sorry. I wasn't thinking. Do you need help finding somewhere to stay while you settle things here?

"No, the caretaker's cottage looks in okay condition. I plan to live there while I renovate the house."

"I can recommend some reliable contractors, and help you get that deed registered. Consider it a welcoming gift."

He didn't need anything from her or anyone else. What he needed was to prove he could rely on himself. Fatigue and a strong desire to change into something that wasn't gritty and smelling of fish overcame him. "Thanks for the offer. I'll get it taken care of. See you around."

Lauren's fading smile softened his dismissal. "Acer and Acer was the executor of Morrison's estate, so I expect you'll be working on it." He threw the words over his shoulder as he forced one foot in front of the other toward his truck.

CHAPTER 2

Lauren shoved the file cabinet drawer closed and tapped the folder she'd removed against her leg. She'd swear that the James Morrison file she held hadn't been there yesterday. Lauren carried it to her office. She'd been working here for nearly a year and didn't know anything about the Morrison estate, hadn't done any research on it for the partners. *Very strange.* She powered on her computer. She knew for a fact that the Morrison file folder on the network had not been there yesterday—at least not on any part of the network she had access to.

She slapped her hand on the desk. But Jesse knew she worked for Acer. His parting words had said so. But he might have gotten that from Annie at court this morning. Had Jesse asked the partners, or whichever partner he was working with, to keep his identity secret, even from the other firm employees? Why? What was he up to? And why was it suddenly not a secret anymore? Had Jesse called, and whoever here was keeping the secret had made the files available by the time she'd gotten back?

Lauren rubbed her temples. She couldn't recall if Jesse had had a cell phone. He hadn't given her a number. The intrigue—most likely imagined on her part—was too much. But wasn't that just like Jesse to whirl in her life like a tornado and upend everything she had carefully, and drama-free, laid out?

The ring of her cell phone startled Lauren and set her heart pounding. Jesse? The pounding slowed. No, her mother. Jesse didn't have her phone number.

"Hi, Mom. What's up?"

"I closed on a nice sale this morning and thought I'd take you to lunch if you're free."

"Congratulations!" Lauren's heart swelled with pride. Moving here from Chenango Falls in Upstate New York a couple of years after Lauren's father had left them was the best thing Mom had ever done. And with no work record, except a part-time job at the makeup counter of a department store for a year and a half, her mother's slide into selling real estate had been a crowning achievement. "Lunch sounds good."

"Caroline's at one? We'll miss the noon crush," her mother said.

"Works for me, and I have some interesting news for you."

"I've got another call I should take. Save it for lunch. See you then."

Lauren flipped open the paper folder and clicked open the Morrison folder on the network. Saving the info that Jesse was in town and the new owner of the Morrison property until lunch was a good idea. It gave her time to learn more and frame what to share with her mother.

A half hour later, she closed both files, not much more informed than when she'd opened them. The information was pretty standard for an estate settlement. But why hadn't the files been in the system before today, and why hadn't she been asked to do the usual deed search and work the partners usually had her do? Lauren rose from her desk and walked out to the reception area. The lights were shut off in both of the guys' offices.

"Brittany," she addressed the office assistant, a woman about her age. "Ray and Gerry are out of the office?" *Duh, of course they were, unless they were sitting in the dark.*

"Yeah, they have a one o'clock tee-time, so they've gone to lunch."

"Right. It's Tuesday."

Brittany laughed.

Their bosses had a standing golf-date on Tuesday with Ken Kostner, one of the largest real estate developers in the Charleston area, the man who owned the real estate office in Indigo Bay that her mother worked for. Lauren checked her phone. 11:50. She had time before lunch with Mom. She should do some real work or at least check her email for some. Her questions about Jesse's inheritance would have to wait.

"I'll catch them later."

"Anything I can help with?" Brittany asked.

"No, thanks." Lauren started to turn back toward her office and stopped. "Maybe. Do you know anything about the Morrison estate? Did you work on it?" Brittany had some paralegal duties.

The woman shook her head. "Did it just come in? The family changed law firms? Mr. Morrison died a couple of years ago."

Foreboding rolled through Lauren. Brittany knew less than she did. "No, the estate was settled six months ago by Acer and Acer."

"Really." Brittany's eyebrows raised with her voice. She tapped something into her computer. "Look at that. There it is. Who knew Ray or Gerry even knew how to enter a client into the system."

Her comment cracked through Lauren's unease and made her smile. The guys weren't what Lauren would call computer savvy. Or was that a good-ole-boy pretense? "I'm going to lunch with my mother at one. If you want to go out now, I'll hold down the fort."

"Great. I do have some errands I wanted to run on my break."

And minding the front desk would give Lauren something to do besides check her email, assuming the firm got any calls. Lately, the workload had her wondering if Ray and Gerry had already ready retired, just hadn't let her and Brittany know yet. Of course, they could have a whole roster of secret clients. She laughed out loud.

She couldn't imagine either of her bosses having the energy or motivation to maintain that kind of intrigue, not to mention the actual legal work. More likely, one of them had taken the Morrison estate because it was simple, despite the family's prominence, former prominence. After the outstanding payments due the facility where Mr. Morrison been for his last years had been paid, all that was left was the real property and a small savings account at the local bank branch. Still, her bosses had kept the information secret from her. What did that say about her position with the firm?

~

Forty-five minutes later, Lauren pushed open the door to Caroline's Café.

"Over here," a deep familiar voice called from a back booth.

The door scraped the side of her leg as she let it go before she was fully inside. There ought to be some cosmic rule about how many times in one day Jesse could surprise her by showing up somewhere she didn't expect him.

The waitress handed her a menu as she passed by. "I'll be with your table in a minute."

"Look who I ran into," her mother said, making room for her to slide into the booth next to her when Lauren made it clear nonverbally that's where she wanted to sit.

"Hi, Mom. Jesse." She settled into the seat, taking care to keep her legs to the side of Jesse's, which he'd stretched out under the table between her and her mother once Lauren was seated.

"After that cinnamon roll you got me this morning, I had to stop by here and try lunch."

Lauren's face heated before she caught the motion of her mother glancing sideways at her.

"You knew Jesse was coming and didn't tell me?" her mother asked.

So, he hadn't been here with Mom long enough to get into the details of their meeting or what had brought him to Indigo Bay.

"No, I was as surprised as you to run into him this morning."

"At City Court," he threw in.

"You're an attorney, too, since your accident?" her mother asked.

"No, I was the defendant and Lauren was my public defender." Jesse laughed as if he were making a joke, but not before Lauren caught a bleak flash in his eyes.

"I got caught sleeping on the beach," he added.

Her mother smiled. *Smiled!*

"It was a beautiful night last, night, but we have to have some rules to keep the desirability and property values up for the tourists."

"Mom's in real estate," Lauren said in response to Jesse's blank look and in hopes of moving the conversation to something else.

Their waitress appeared at the booth to help her mission. "Are you ready to order?"

"I am," Lauren's mother said. "I'll have the seafood cobb salad. House dressing on the side and iced tea."

Lauren was next. "I'll have the same. Blue cheese dressing on the side and raspberry iced tea.

The waitress, a young woman Lauren didn't know, jotted down the order and turned her full attention to Jesse. "And you, sir," the waitress said in a sugary sweet accent that hadn't sounded close to as thick when she'd addressed Lauren and her mother.

Curling and relaxing her fingers, Lauren waited for the waitress to bat her lashes at him. What did she care if the woman did? She had no claim on Jesse. Hadn't for years, if ever.

"Sonja," he nodded at Lauren's mother, "recommended the pulled pork sandwich platter."

Sonja. When had Jesse and his mother moved to a first-name basis? In all the time she'd know him, he'd called her mother Mrs. Cooper. She glanced at her mother, who had no reaction to Jesse using her first name. Mom had run hot and cold on Jesse—her and Jesse, not that there was any her and Jesse—depending on how much money he was pulling in. Of course, Jesse might have told Mom about his inheritance.

"And would y'all like regular or sweet potato fries with that?" the waitress asked.

"Sweet potato, definitely," Jesse answered with a wide grin that wasn't quite the smile she thought of as hers, but close.

Lauren grabbed her napkin and concentrated on opening it and smoothing it on her lap. The waitress *had* batted her eyelashes at his response.

"And coffee, black." He finished his order.

Lauren raised her head to the waitress' retreating back. "So," she said too brightly, "have you told Mom your big news, what brought you to Indigo Bay?"

Jesse shifted in the booth. "I'm going to renovate the Morrison place."

Her mother's eyes lit up. "You bought it? I've always thought it would be a perfect B&B."

That was Mom's latest dream, to open a B&B, and she might do it someday. Lauren's mood softened. Mom had come a long way from the woman who'd been one hundred percent dependent on Lauren's father a few years ago, before she'd moved south.

"I didn't exactly buy it," Jesse said.

"I see. You're the contractor. So who owns it? The whole town has been speculating on that. I showed the property six months or so ago. It has a lot of potential, but needs tons of work.

Interesting. Jesse had had the house on the market, but changed his mind.

"The property, the house was for sale?" Jesse pursed his lips as though he hadn't mean to ask his question out loud.

"Yes, the word around the office was that executor had problems locating the heir, so the property was listed, I assume to keep the maintenance on the property from draining the estate's cash."

Jesse mumbled what sounded like, "What cash?"

Lauren checked her mother's face for a reaction. She must not have heard him.

"I had a good offer, considering the condition, but the listing was yanked before it was accepted. I assume that's when the heir was found and that he or she didn't want to sell."

A series of undecipherable emotions played across Jesse's face, ending in relief when the café's owner Caroline approached the table with their lunches.

"Hi, I didn't see you come in. I know this cobb salad is yours, Sonja, and I assume the pulled pork if for …" Her voice drifted off, waiting for an introduction.

"Jesse, Jesse Brewster," Lauren's mother got in before she could make the introduction. "My good friend, Caroline Harper."

"Ah, of the cinnamon rolls fame," he said. "Nice to meet you."

"You, too. You're a friend of Lauren's?"

The glint in her mother's friend's eyes as she gave Jesse a once over told Lauren what Caroline probably was thinking. She shouldn't be surprised. She'd grown up in another small town where people were quick to put others together as a couple. And she wasn't even going to try to figure out why that sowed a flower-pot seed of emptiness in her.

"Former co-workers," he said.

That was all they were? The seed blossomed into a crater. She stabbed a leaf of lettuce and almost sent a cherry tomato sailing across the table. She shouldn't care. Change that to didn't care. He'd lied to her. He'd said he'd wait.

"You remember," Lauren's mother said. "Lauren worked at the Team Macachek racing headquarters when she was going to Syracuse University."

On school vacations, she'd been the cleaning crew for the lodging the team owned for the members whenever they were at the headquarters or needed somewhere to stay when they were between races. She'd expected Jesse to go there when he'd recovered from his accident. He hadn't.

"You're one of the racers," Caroline said.

"I was."

His flat intonation tugged at Lauren's heart. Racing hadn't been just Jesse's career. It had been his life.

Caroline smoothed her apron. "So, you're retired. I read somewhere that racers often retire in their late twenties or early thirties. Must be nice, but I can't imagine what I'd do if I didn't have the café to keep me busy."

Her mother opened her mouth to speak and Lauren held her breath that Mom wasn't going to say Jesse had been forced to stop racing. If he'd wanted Caroline to know about his accident, he would have told her.

"Jesse is going to have plenty to keep him busy. He's been hired to renovate the Morrison place," her mother said.

Lauren's breath whooshed out.

"You don't say. Then, Jesse, you must know who the new mystery owner is."

Before Jesse could answer, their waitress rushed out of the kitchen. "Caroline. We need you in the kitchen. There's a problem with the delivery."

Caroline sighed. "I'd better go. You can fill me in later, Sonja. And before I forget, if you haven't sent in your reservation for the college reunion, do it today. I don't want to go and not know anyone there."

"Mom and Caroline were college roommates at the University of South Carolina." Lauren bit her tongue. College was a sore spot with Jesse, or it had been. But, for all she knew about his past few years, he could have gone back and completed three degrees.

"Yep, back in the dark ages. Caroline invited me here for a visit a few years ago, and I never left."

Jesse's expression turned thoughtful. "And you followed for law school."

"Pretty much. Carolina gave me a good financial aid package." Lauren wasn't about to tell him that was only half the reason, that he was the other half. "After Dad sold the house and Mom left Chenango Falls, I didn't anything much to keep me there,"

Jesse dropped his gaze to his plate as if deciding whether to have the last bite of his sandwich or dig into the remaining fries was a decision that required all of his attention. He glanced at the clock on the wall. "I'd better get going, too. I have a 2:15 appointment to make. I'm sure I'll see you ladies around."

Lauren watched Jesse stride across the café, flirt with both their waitress and the woman on the cash register, and exit the building. Had her dig about nothing to stick around for struck a nerve? Her heart rate ticked up. Had it brought up feelings that made him walk away rather than face her? She stared out the glass door and reined in the tempo of her heart beat. It couldn't have. She was placing importance on nothing He'd simply finished his lunch and had an appointment to make. The Jesse she'd known didn't walk away from anything.

Jesse had to bite the side of his mouth to keep himself from laughing at the expression on Lauren's face when Brittany walked him into Lauren's office.

"This is Mr. Brewster. He had a 2:15 appointment with Ray that apparently Ray forgot to reschedule when that other … thing came up."

The other thing being golfing with his brother and Ken Kostner. Early this morning, Ray Acer had texted him an invitation to join them. Jesse had declined. But he'd kept the appointment, knowing Lauren would be the only lawyer in. It hadn't taken any effort at all to convince Brittany to let him consult with Lauren in Ray's place.

"It's about the Morrison estate we were talking about earlier," Brittany said.

"I know what it's about. Come in, Jesse. Take a seat."

Brittany stepped back through the doorway and pulled the office door closed behind her, but not before she'd looked from him to Lauren and ended her perusal with a grin and a raised eyebrow.

Only in his dreams.

"You're here to retitle your property, as we talked about this morning," Lauren said, all business.

"Yeah, that too." He'd wanted to get her alone, so they could really talk, but was starting to wimp out. What was there to talk about? The past was over and done with.

She frowned as she waited for him to take a seat.

He curled the fingers of his left hand around the top of the chair back and leaned his weight onto it to cover the loss of feeling and sudden weakness in his right foot. A glance told him Lauren hadn't noticed. She was already bringing up a form on her computer. His pride sighed in relief, while another part of him that he kept locked away ached with wanting to shout, *there's a good reason I stayed away. I'm not the man you wanted anymore.*

Her fingers flew over the keys. "Current address. Your dad's in California?"

"No, the caretaker's place on Uncle Jim's property. Does it have a separate address from the main house? That would be something I'd need to know."

Avoiding his gaze, she minimized the form and opened a document. From where he was sitting, he couldn't see around the edge of the computer screen to read it. But he could study her profile, the way she bit her lower lip when she was concentrating—or trying to block something out. Him? He didn't know whether to be hurt or flattered that he still affected her. Not that it mattered. Lauren had always been out of his league, even more so now that she was a lawyer.

Lauren closed that document and went to an internet map. Probably the town or county tax map. "Here it is. The property has been subdivided." She ripped a post-it note off her pad and wrote on it. "The cottage's address."

Lauren handed him the note, taking care not to let her fingers brush his. Or was that wishful thinking on his part?

"I'm surprised Ray didn't go over that at the reading of the will."

"We've done everything by mail, my lawyer and I. Mac offered me the services of the team lawyer, even though …" Jesse paused. "Even though I'm not racing anymore."

He dropped his gaze to the post-it note as if to memorize the address. *Nice going, Brewster.* She'd think he couldn't afford his own lawyer, which he couldn't. He didn't even need his own attorney. Mac Macachek, the racing team owner and his former boss, had suggested it when Jesse had mentioned receiving the letters from Acer and Acer. After his mother's death and the bender he'd gone on for far too long afterwards, Jesse hadn't been in any frame of mind to read through the documents the law firm had sent him.

"I've never met either of your partners," he said.

"I'm not a partner."

"Yet," he said, not doubting that was her plan, nor that she'd achieve it.

Something flickered in Lauren's eyes. Uncertainty? She was the most confident person he knew. Or make that had known. Of course, he didn't know what her life had been the past few years. And could only hope she didn't know what his had been.

"I'll have the deed change recorded with the county." Lauren was back to business. "I'm surprised Ray hasn't taken care of it." She pressed a finger to her lips as if she wanted to take back her last words and creased her brows.

The team lawyer had told Jesse that Acer and Acer was the biggest law firm in Indigo Bay—he wouldn't have expected anything less for Lauren—and had expressed surprise that the firm had taken so long to locate Jesse. Uncle Jim's will had been simple and specific, everything was to go to Jesse's mother and to Jesse if his mother died before Uncle Jim. Mom and Dad's home address hadn't changed from the one Uncle Jim had in the will until his dad had moved into the rental condo. Jesse had figured the firm had bigger cases to deal with, more important things to do than track him down. That was before Jesse had checked out the beachfront property values in Indigo Bay and learned how prominent the Morrison family had been here.

"Thanks," he said. "And if I have any more questions, I can call you?"

"Ray's the attorney of record. You should call him."

Ah, there was the brush off he'd been expecting. But she had offered to help him register the deed. What had happened between this morning and now? Maybe she had done a search on what he had and hadn't been doing since his accident.

Lauren finished at the computer and leaned back in her chair. "We'd be happy to serve as your real estate attorney."

Jesse pinned her gaze with his.

She blinked and broke the contact. "That's your plan, isn't it? To renovate the mansion and sell it?"

"Yeah, that's the plan."

"Then, back to California and the bike shop?"

He gripped the chair arms. "Dad sold the shop to pay Mom's medical bills."

She looked as if he'd slapped her. "I ... I'm sorry. I had no idea."

So she hadn't Googled him. His stomach clenched. What was with him? He should be glad. "It's okay. He's getting used to being semi-retired, doing custom work for a couple shops. He's got a new condo." Jesse stopped himself from telling her, Dad had had to sell the house, too. "As for me ..." Jesse made sure he had Lauren's full attention for the real reason he'd come. "I have my eye on the old gas station property on Seaside Boulevard your mother told me about for setting up my own custom bike shop after I finish the mansion renovation."

CHAPTER 3

"Lauren, could I see you in my office?" Ray ordered as much as asked through the phone.

She hung up and pushed away from her desk, hoping her boss had something for her to work on—anything to work on. She'd spent the time since she'd arrived this morning neatening her office and replaying yesterday from her first seeing Jesse at the jail to him striding out of her office. She should have asked him why Indigo Bay and a lot of other questions while he was here. But she'd assured him Mom knew her business, said goodbye, and watched him leave.

She rubbed her temples. Was that really only yesterday?

Ray was frowning and tapping his fingers on the desk when she walked in.

"Brittany said you met with Jesse Brewster yesterday."

Lauren eyed the chair in front of her boss's desk, gauging whether their conversation would be long enough for her to sit. She opted for the leverage of standing. "Yes, he said he had a 2:15 appointment with you, but you and Gerry were golf …"

Ray's eyes narrowed.

"You were out of the office. Mr. Brewster asked to see someone else."

"And you volunteered?"

What was with Ray's third degree? "Jesse asked about the title to the Morrison house. He said he hadn't received an updated deed with the property distribution."

"Jesse, is it?"

Lauren straightened to her full height. "Yes, it turns out our new, or new-to-me at least, client is someone I knew back in New York."

"I see," he said with none of the Southern charm in his voice he generally used with all women, even her and Brittany.

This conversation was getting weirder and weirder.

"I saw the new client file on the network yesterday morning and read through it. Since the estate has already been probated, I filed the updated deed electronically with the county while Jesse was here."

Ray made a choking sound.

Lauren rushed over and patted his back. "Are you all right?" He *had* had a heart attack last year.

"I'm fine." Ray pushed her hand away, muttering what sounded like *it was none of your business*. "Brewster just called me."

Then, why had Ray grilled her when he could have asked Jesse?

"Evidently, he's lost the key to the shed on the property. He claimed he never got it, but it was sent to him with the other keys. I need you to run this spare key over to him."

"Can't Brittany do it?" Lauren tried to come up with a business reason she couldn't.

Ray's frown deepened. "He asked for you. Keep the client happy. Ken Kostner is interested in buying the property from Brewster. You might want to drop that bit of information, along with the key."

So that was the client Ray wanted to keep happy. Lauren held her hand out for the key, and Ray dropped it in her hand.

"And stop by the Post Office for the mail on your way back," Ray said.

Annoyance edged up her spine. That was one of Brittany's duties. But she was going out anyway, and Ray knew her schedule was light—or more accurately— empty. "Sure," she forced out. And she would tell Jesse about Ken's interest in the mansion property. As far as she could tell, Jesse could use the sales proceeds. Mom could make a killing on the sale. And if Jesse wasn't stuck here fixing up the property, he might give up the idea opening his bike shop in Indigo Bay. Her life could go back to normal. No Jesse tornados. No pick up the pieces after he blew back out of town.

Since Ray hadn't seemed in any hurry to have her back in the office, Lauren chose to walk to the beach, hoping the bright warm morning sun would burn off the malaise that thoughts of her normal life had brought. She kicked a stone off the sidewalk. She had a good life. A calm, planned life, with the opportunity to head the largest law firm in town once Ray and Gerry retired. Lauren smiled to herself. A life Jesse, as usual, had disrupted. But as attractive a disruption as he was, he was a disruption she couldn't afford to get caught up in.

Lauren halted her thoughts and feet at the gate opening to the Morrison mansion's driveway. An Indigo Bay police cruiser was parked near the caretaker's house, which was originally the gatehouse. An officer and another person blocked by the officer stood talking with Jesse. She strode down the drive.

"And here's my lawyer if you need further proof," Jesse said when she got within hearing range near the caretaker's cottage.

What had he gotten himself into now?

"Hi, Ben," she said to the officer, pursing her lips as she recognized the perfectly coiffed, impeccably dressed senior citizen standing next to him. Lucille Sanderson, the biggest busybody in town holding her fluffy white dog, whose jade green collar matched her jade green espadrilles.

"Lauren."

"Is there a problem?" she asked.

"A misunderstanding," Ben said, exchanging an amused glance with Jesse.

"I was taking a walk on the beach and saw this man breaking into a shed," Lucille interjected, pointing at Jesse. "I called Officer Andrews and stood behind a bush until he arrived."

Lauren covered her smile with her hand. The espadrilles must be Lucille's casual concession to her usual heels for walking on the beach.

"Walking on my beach," Jesse added. "And my shed."

Lauren glared at Jesse. He was purposely egging the older woman on.

"So he really does own the Morrison house?" Lucille demanded of Lauren. "I heard the estate had finally been settled."

That's why Lucille had been walking on the beach. She was pretty sure she'd never seen the woman beach walking before.

"Yes, Lucille, he does," Lauren said.

"You'll be staying here in town?" Lucille asked.

"I will." The way the corners of Jesse's mouth twitched belied the seriousness of his tone. "In the caretaker's cottage while I renovate the big house."

Lucille studied him. "You'll want to meet some young people. I'll introduce you to my great niece Maggie."

Lucille was constantly trying to fix up Maggie, who'd come to visit Indigo Bay last summer and stayed, not that Lauren could see that the woman needed any help in that department.

"I appreciate that, but I already know Lauren from when we both lived in Upstate New York. She's offered to show me around town."

No, no, no! Lauren wanted to shout. On two counts. Lucille would spread all around town that she and Jesse were old "friends." And she'd said nothing about showing him around town. Her plan, not that she was succeeding with it, had been to have as little contact as possible with him.

Ben's phone beeped. He glanced at the screen. "I've got to get back to the station. Lucille, would you like a ride home?"

"A ride back to my car near the Boardwalk would be nice. I've tired Princess out with our longer than usual walk today."

"It was nice to meet you, Lucille," Jesse said.

"Yes, once I found out you weren't a criminal. I'll get back to you about meeting Maggie."

"Yes, you do that," he said.

"You shouldn't encourage her," Lauren said once Ben and Lucille were in the cruiser.

He shrugged, nicking her temper.

"By lunchtime, everyone in Indigo Bay will be speculating whether we're just old friends or old *friends*."

"No harm, we are. Both." The teasing expression left Jesse face. "Or maybe you're ashamed of our connection."

"Of course not." The cinnamon roll she'd splurged on for breakfast sat heavy in her stomach. Or was she? She'd come to Indigo Bay after law school to make a new start. It was a good place for doing that. Look at Mom. That seemed to be what Jesse wanted to do, too. Who was she to stand in his way?

"You know making like we're a couple, won't stop Lucille from trying to fix you up with her niece," Lauren said in what she hoped sounded like a tease.

"Does that bother you?"

"No, why should it?" A flashback to the winter of her sophomore year of college replayed her showing him how to drive a snowmobile and him promising to take her to his Southern California home and show her how to surf. Her mind fast forwarded to the Indigo Bay beach and Jesse in Hawaiian print swim trunks riding low on his lean hips showing Maggie how to surf, the sun glinting off the sun-bleached ends of his close-cropped light brown hair.

It shouldn't bother her, but it did.

~

Jesse wanted to take his taunt back. He wanted to kiss the changing expressions on Lauren's face into a smile before they settled on disgust. He wanted all kinds of things he couldn't have. He watched Lauren compose herself and followed her gaze to the shed behind him. The doors stood open. He'd unscrewed the simple hasp hardware when he couldn't unlock the padlock.

"You couldn't have waited for the key?" Lauren dangled the keyring in the air.

"I got back from beach clean-up and wanted to get to work here." *Which will be a lot easier if the tools I need were in the shed, and I didn't have to go buy them.* He had about every mechanical engine tool known to man, but not what he needed for home repair and grounds maintenance.

"And you couldn't find the key."

"I never had the key." Jesse wasn't proud of the haze he'd used to create distance between himself and Lauren, himself and life, long after his accident and his mother's death. But it made no sense to him that he had every other key the house and grounds, but that one.

"Fortunately, we had another one," she contradicted him.

"You don't believe I never had a key?" Of course his dropping off the face of the earth to her and most everyone else after his accident didn't give a lot of credence to his part of the promise to wait for each other they'd made when she was in college and his motocross career was taking off. "And you don't think it's odd that Ray happened to have an extra key to the property, even though the estate's been settled?"

Her eyes widened, and her mouth opened in an O, followed by nervous foot tapping.

"Ha, you did think it's odd."

"I'm sure the extra key just somehow got overlooked."

"That doesn't say a lot for Acer and Acer. Want to see what they kept access to? Officer Andrews arrived before I got a look."

Lauren pinched her lips together.

He took a step toward the open doors. He didn't know when to shut up. But acting like he was would discourage Lauren from any thoughts that there was still, could be, anything between them. She was out of his league socially and intellectually, always had been, and he wasn't going to let her forget that. He'd hurt her enough in the past by believing and letting her believe the fairy tale of their relationship. He closed the distance to the shed. Who was he kidding? Lauren hadn't shown any renewed interest in him. His protections were all to contain the attraction he still felt toward her.

Jesse shivered at the drop in temperature and loss of sunlight when he walked into the stone building. He wrinkled his nose at the dank smell and reached back to the left for the light switch he'd seen. Only his hand touched neither the expected switch or the stone wall he expected but, rather, something soft.

Lauren's gasp accelerated the buzz of electricity that had already burned halfway through him.

"Uh. Sorry. The light."

"Yeah, you could use some light in here." She flicked the switch and the single bulb above lit.

"I didn't do that on purpose," he stammered when he found his voice. "I didn't know you were behind me."

"Good to know." Her voice was as dry as the sunbaked sand out on the beach.

Jesse adjusted his eyes to the dimly lighted interior and flexed the fingers of his left hand. No danger of her falling for him again. His stomach churned. Nothing but black coffee for breakfast might not have been the best idea. But keeping Lauren at a distance was what he wanted, especially if they were going to be living in the same small town.

"What are you looking for in here?" Lauren asked.

"Gold bullion," he tossed back. Any equipment and tools he could use so he didn't have to buy them would be about as good.

"You're not back on Ray and the key, are you?" Exasperation crept into her voice.

"No, I … never mind." A faint floral scent broke through the mustiness. Lauren's hair? Perfume? The shed looked larger from the outside, or had her close proximity made it feel small now that they were alone inside it? "Don't you have to get back to work?" he asked.

She walked around and stood in front of him.

The floral scent was stronger, and he recognized it, remembered burying his face in her long blond hair and breathing it in. Jesse clenched and unclenched his fists.

"I should. I have to stop at the post office and it closes for lunch from 10:45 to 11:45 so they can be open during regular lunch-time hours. Before I go, though, I have a proposition for you."

Jesse cleared his throat. He was certain her proposition wasn't the one he was resisting making to her. "What's that?"

"If you're anxious to get your bike shop up and running here or somewhere else."

The way Lauren emphasized the *or somewhere else*, made Jesse think she might not be as indifferent to him as he'd thought. He shook his head. *No.* Indifference was good.

"Don't say no say until I finish."

"Huh?" He hadn't said anything.

"I have a lead on a buyer for the Morrison house, your house. As is, so you wouldn't have to spend your time renovating it. Good money."

Jesse laughed without mirth. Lauren wasn't indifferent to him. She just plain wanted him gone from Indigo Bay. "You can't get rid of me that easily."

"I'm not trying to get rid of you. I just thought, your dad, people you know are in Southern California."

"There's nothing there for me. If things work out here, I'm going to ask Dad to come and work with me. Besides, I've already made a gentleman's agreement to sell the place."

"You talked to Ray?"

"No, to your mother. We're going in on it together. Her money. My muscle." Jesse flexed his biceps Incredible Hulk style.

Lauren's gasp of surprise was even better than he'd expected.

~

Lauren stomped into the post office. The walk from the beach hadn't fully taken the edge off her irritation. Her mother couldn't have the kind of money it would take to buy the Morrison house. Or could she? Lauren hadn't handled her mother's finances since Mom had moved here. Mom had said Caroline was helping her to manage them herself. But the mortgage on the duplex Mom had bought, where Lauren rented the other side of the house, had to be pretty steep, even if the property only had a view of the ocean and not beach frontage.

She got in line behind a stunning brunette she didn't recognize. But with all the tourists in and out of the area, that wasn't surprising.

"I'm sorry," the post office clerk said. "I can't give you Mr. Brewster's address."

The woman was looking for Jesse? Lauren didn't know any other Brewsters in Indigo Bay. She checked out the woman more thoroughly. The woman didn't look like a motocross groupie. But then her friend and second cousin Sari in Chenango Falls wasn't the typical picture of a motocross groupie, and Sari was crazy about motocross. Besides, Jesse hadn't raced in three years. The woman could be someone Jesse had had a real relationship with. Lauren breathed in a deep breath to combat the sinking feeling growing inside her. Jesse had been faithful to her when they were dating. What he'd done after they'd drifted apart wasn't her concern.

The woman's shoulders drooped and then stiffened. "Thanks for nothing." She turned and glared at Lauren, as if saying *what are you looking at?* before marching out the door.

"Hi, Lauren," the clerk said, reaching under the counter and lifting a small packet of mail. "Brittany off today?"

"No, I had to go meet with a client at his home, so I thought I'd save Brittany the trip and pick up the mail on my way back to the office." *Or, more accurately, Ray thought he'd show me my place by ordering me to stop for the mail.*

The clerk handed Lauren the mail. "Here you go. That woman was asking about the guy who inherited the Morrison property. Some distant relative from California."

"Yes, Jim Morrison's grandnephew." Lauren bit her tongue.

"Yeah, you'd know that. You guys probably did the estate. I'm fine giving directions if someone asks how to get to an address. But we can't give out a person's address to anyone who walks in. Regulations."

Lauren pulled a wry smile. But the clerk could gossip with locals, and she'd added to that by mentioning Jesse's relationship to Mr. Morrison. "Thanks." She lifted the packet of envelopes as a goodbye wave, turned, and almost ran into her mother.

"Lauren. I thought that was you." Her mother's gaze dropped to Lauren's hand. "Brittany off today?"

"No."

"I would think Ray and Gerry would have better use for your time than the morning mail run."

The packet of mail crackled as Lauren's fingers tightened around it. Having a law degree didn't preclude her from picking up the firm's mail. It didn't mean anything. Ray and Gerry sometimes stopped at the post office if they were going out of the office.

"I had to drop off a key to Jesse. He'd misplaced the one to the equipment shed."

"Good, he's getting right to work."

"About that …"

"Hey, Sonja, the post office clerk said. "Here for your mail?"

"Go ahead." Lauren waved toward the counter. The whole town didn't need to know what she had to say to her mother.

"See you tomorrow," her mother said and rejoined Lauren by the door.

"Did you drive?" Lauren asked.

"No, I walked."

"Good, we can walk back to our offices together." She pushed to door open for the two of them.

Her mother slipped through the door ahead of her. "And you can tell me what had your face all puckered up in there."

"Nothing. That's not what I wanted to talk with you about."

Her mother made what was as close to an unladylike sound as she ever came.

"All right, this woman, not from around here, was in the post office asking for Jesse's address. And I inadvertently dropped that Mr. Morrison's grandnephew had inherited the property," Lauren added so her mother wouldn't get the idea that another woman asking about Jesse would bother her—even if it had bothered her.

"The stunning brunette with the attitude? She dropped in the real estate office first thing this morning asking about our recent sales and rentals as if she was checking out our services and record. But I saw through her, picked up that she was looking for information. Information she could find in the public records at the county building."

"Mom, you didn't tell her that?"

"Of course not," her mother dismissed her question. "I thought I'd mention her to Jesse. If he wants her to know where he is, he can tell her."

"Speaking of Jesse ..." Who, given that her intention was to avoid him, was taking up far too much of her life, even when he wasn't around in person. "Did you really agree to buy the mansion, to go into business with him?"

"We haven't signed an agreement yet."

Lauren sighed a silent sigh of relief. She had time to stop her mother's fantasy before Mom got hurt personally and financially.

"But I sure plan to. I'm writing an agreement as soon as I get back to the office."

Lauren touched her mother's arm. "Buying and renovating the mansion into a B&B is a big and expensive undertaking. He hasn't said in so many words, but I think he's strapped for cash."

"Exactly why we're partnering."

Lauren stopped and put her hands on her hips. "Where is the money coming from? You should have talked with me before you agreed to anything with Jesse. At least, it's not in writing yet."

"Honey, I know you like to help, and there's no way I can ever make up to you for taking care of me in so many ways after your father left. But I haven't needed your financial guidance and help since I went to work here at the real estate office."

"But the duplex. You have a mortgage." She couldn't fathom how her mother could finance something as big as she and Jesse planned.

"A very manageable one, even without your rent. I used part of what I got on the sale of our old house in Chenango Falls as a down payment and invested the rest. I took that community education class in investing at the high school. Remember?"

Lauren remembered. She'd had no idea her mother was serious about investing. She had taken numerous community ed classes to meet people here, or so Lauren had thought. "I remember."

"Well I applied what I learned and have done okay. Add in those couple big sales I've made this year, and I think Jesse and I can do it." Sonja raised her hand, index finger up. "And before you say anything about renting property being different than selling property, I've already picked Caroline's son Dallas' brain. He has a lot of experience with his seaside cottages.

The right words wouldn't come. She should be proud of her mother She *was* proud of her. All she could think, though was *no one needs me*. The firm had barely enough work to keep Ray and Gerry busy.

Against her will, she pictured the attractive woman asking about Jesse at the Post Office. He hadn't needed her in years. Her independent mother didn't need her help anymore.

"I'll want you to look over the contract before Jesse and I sign it."

"Sure." A concession to make her feel better? She shook off the poor-little-me attitude. She handled all of her mother's legal matters. This wasn't any different.

Her phone rang. Most people texted her, except Ray and Gerry. "I'd better answer. It might be the office."

Her mother nodded.

It was an unknown number. "Hello."

"Hi. You're my attorney, right?" What sounded like a small child crying almost drowned out Jesse's voice.

He didn't wait for her to answer. "I need you here. Now. Please."

CHAPTER 4

"Oomph." Jesse took a hard kick to the thigh from the now screaming kid who'd been shoved into his arms by a woman he'd never met before. Clutching the kid, he crouched to retrieve his cell phone he'd dropped in the process. As soon as the woman had gotten out of the car and shouted "Jesse Brewster, here's your kid," he'd speed dialed Lauren's cell phone number. Brittany had given it to him the other day with no questions. For business, of course.

The woman faced off with him. "She's not mine, and I won't be responsible for her. I put in my responsible time with her mother, for all it got me. Since she has a father, I'd rather not see her in foster care like Crystal and me. I told her from the start she should make you acknowledge the baby, hit you up for support."

"Hold it. Who's your sister? Crystal who? From where?" His gaze drilled into the woman's and queasiness overcame him when he really looked at her features. He pulled his gaze away to study the child he held and looked into his mother's wide eyes, saw her pert nose and a cupid version of his mother's mouth. He smoothed the little girl's hair absently. Hair the same shade of sandy brown as his and his mother's. Bile rose in his throat. That hazy time after his accident when he'd learned his racing career was over and had broken off contact with Lauren. His mother had been dying, and there hadn't been anything he could do. He'd had an insane need to prove he wasn't useless, was still a man.

"Where is your sister?" he asked.

"Dead. Everything you need to know is in the front pocket of the suitcase with the kid's stuff." The woman placed the case on the driveway and took a step back toward her car.

Jesse rubbed the heel of his palm against his chest. This little girl's whole life was in a suitcase. "Wait." He matched the woman's step, as if sticking with her would stop her from reaching the car. "My lawyer will be here any minute." Or, at least he hoped she would be. The cell phone's tumble from his hands had ended the call.

"Good. He can help you." The woman pushed the case toward him and took advantage of the distraction to escape to her car and hop in."

He rushed after her. She fired up the engine. "Stop." He couldn't grab the door handle and put the kid in danger.

She pulled away and sped down the driveway.

"You didn't tell me her name," he said to the departing taillights.

"Aunt Tara's gone. Mommy's gone," the little girl sniffed.

"I'm afraid so." She had no idea how afraid. He hugged her to his chest. "I'm Jesse," he said into her hair."

The little girl pushed away and looked him in the eye. "Aunt Tara said Daddy."

He patted her awkwardly on the back. "We'll see," he muttered. "What's your name?"

"Shelley."

He swallowed hard. His mother's name.

A car slowed down at the open gate by the road. Had Aunt Tara had second thoughts and returned? A different vehicle he didn't recognize drove toward him and stopped.

Lauren got out of the driver's side and her mother the passenger side.

"What do we have here?" Sonja asked.

He'd swear Lauren had said, "A big problem is my guess" under her breath. But that may have been his own inner voice of doom.

Sonja strode over. "Isn't she precious?"

Jesse's heart swelled. She was. "This is Shelley."

"Hi, Shelley. I'm Sonja."

"Gama?" the little girl said, reaching her arms to Lauren's mother.

He let Sonja take Shelley, his gaze connecting with Lauren's unreadable one. His jaw tightened. Her lawyer expression. What had he expected, her to leap for joy that he might have a child?

Lauren broke the connection and frowned at her mother. For not correcting Shelley?

"Jesse-Daddy." Shelley pointed at him.

With extreme effort, he attempted a casual shrug and mouthed "maybe" at Lauren.

Liar, his heart screamed. *You know she's yours.* His child. The grandchild his mother had looked forward to having. A child both he and his mother had expected would be with Lauren. His eyes stung and his head clogged.

"I see," Sonja said, studying the little girl's face. She tapped her nose playfully. "I know Jesse."

She left off the Daddy part, but he heard it loud and clear, as he was sure Lauren did, too.

"Mommy gone. Aunt Tara gone," Shelley repeated.

"You poor darling," Sonja snugged Shelley with none of the awkwardness he'd had. "Why don't we sit down to talk?" When neither he nor Lauren said anything, Sonja tugged Lauren to a weather-beaten ornate wrought iron bench.

Jesse followed, an unexpected depression in the ground triggering the unpredictable weakness in his foot. He glanced at Lauren and Sonja. They hadn't noticed his almost-stumble. But he'd caught Sonja's moral support. Was she supporting him because of their business deal? A deal that wasn't final. He closed that hallway in his mind. He was way in over his head and would take help wherever offered.

Lauren and her mother sat, one at each end of the bench as if Lauren didn't want to be too close to Shelley. He stood resting his hand on the bench back near her and flexed his ankle.

"Jesse, you sit, too," Sonja said.

His innate obstinance told him to say *no I'll stand.* But his ankle could use to have the weight off it for a while.

"Jesse-Daddy sit," Shelley repeated.

He wedged himself between the two women, trying unsuccessfully to avoid having his whole left side touching Lauren.

"Good boy." Shelley said, bringing a smile to even Lauren's face.

Shelly scrambled onto his lap and touched his stubbled cheek. With her on his lap and Lauren so close next to him, it was a double-teamed effort to rob the whole atmosphere—or at least the part he had access to—of oxygen.

"Tell me what happened." Lauren's no-nonsense tone counteracted Shelley's stroking his cheek, and Jesse choked in a big breath.

He glanced from Lauren to Shelley to Sonja and back to Lauren. "Uh, little ears." Even in her lawyer armor, Lauren had to know that hearing them talk about her and her aunt was apt to upset Shelley.

"Shelley, sweetie. Do you want to pick flowers with me?" Sonja asked, pointing to a clump of flowers growing in wild disorder by the steps to the caretaker's house about fifty feet away.

"Yellow," Shelley said, disentangling herself from Jesse.

"Yes, yellow jasmine." Sonja led her away, Jesse's gaze following.

Lauren cleared her throat, and he looked away.

"Scoot down, and tell me what's going on." She took a tablet from her bag and turned it on.

As much as he was getting comfortable with Lauren pressed to his side, he moved away so she could let go of the stiff brittle way she'd held herself since he'd sat down.

With frequent glances toward Sonja and Shelley, he told Lauren about Shelley's aunt catching him outside tinkering with the ancient lawn tractor, trying to get it running to mow the lawn.

"You didn't lock the front gate?" she asked.

"I didn't know they locked. I thought they were for decoration." He anticipated his aw-shucks, what-do-I-know attitude would get him a smile from Lauren. It didn't.

"What did the woman look like?"

"Not too tall. Dark hair, long. Kind of hot."

Lauren typed on the tablet, her mouth drawn in a thin line. "You'd recognize her again?"

A shriek from Shelley had him on the edge of the bench ready to stand.

"It's okay," Sonja shouted. "She saw a butterfly."

He waved to the two of them.

"You'd recognize her again?" Lauren repeated, her question grating against his patience. Where was the warm Lauren he'd fallen for as a teen and all over again at twenty?

"Yeah, I know who she is."

"You know her?"

"No, I know who she is. I hooked up with her sister a couple of times." The expression that flashed on Lauren's face pinched his heart. But what was with her interrogation? All he wanted was to find out what he needed to do legally to accept his responsibilities. "Tara, the aunt, said everything I needed to know is in the suitcase."

Lauren's response tore through him like a ballistic missile. "Good, Child Protective Services will need that when they come to pick her up."

White hot anger radiated from Jesse, who'd bolted from the bench to loom over her. "That wasn't exactly my plan."

Lauren pressed back in the bench to get away from the heat. "I, I …" She what? She didn't really know. Wanted to strike back at Jesse for seeing other women? That was nonsense. After Jesse had left her, she'd almost become engaged to her law school boyfriend.

He strode over and retrieved the suitcase as if he had to be doing something physical, returning to the bench with a sheaf of papers in his hand.

Jesse glanced from the top sheet to her. I'm ninety-nine percent sure she's my daughter. Jesse glanced from the top sheet to her. I'm ninety-nine percent sure she's my daughter. She has my mother's first name, looks like pictures of my mother at her age, and the timing is right for her birthdate." He handed her Shelley's birth certificate.

He handed her Shelley's birth certificate.

"But you're not listed as the father. You didn't sign a Paternity Acknowledgement Affidavit." She fell back on doing her legal job, explaining the situation.

He paced in front of her. "I didn't even know she existed."

"Sit down, please."

He dropped to the bench with a force that shook the bench. And her.

"You said you called me as your attorney. I'm just explaining the legal situation."

Jesse set his jaw as he listened.

"The Department of Social Services will take care of her while they establish paternity,"

"Foster care?" he asked.

"Yes."

"I called you as a friend, too, not just my lawyer."

"I am your friend." She reached to touch his hand, and he jumped up again, leaving her touching empty air.

"No kid of mine is going into foster care."

"You don't know she's your daughter. It's better if she doesn't get attached to you if she's not.

"*You* don't know she isn't," he shot back. The fire left his eyes and they softened to a look he'd once had for her. "I knew she was mine from the minute she said her name is Shelley. She looks just like pictures of my mom as a kid."

Lauren knew how close Jesse had been to his mother, how much he must miss her. She couldn't let him accept a child as his because he hadn't gotten over his mother's death.

"We need a potty," Lauren's mother interrupted before she could frame the right words to say to Jesse.

"The cottage is open. I'll show you," he said.

Her mother glanced at the birth certificate and other papers Jesse had in his hand. "No, just tell us. I'll take her while you and Lauren finish talking.

"It's off the kitchen. Once you get inside ..." He gave the directions and continued to look toward the cottage as they walked away, Shelly hopping from foot to foot.

"They'll be fine," Lauren said to get his attention. "Can I look at the other documents you have?"

"What? Yeah." He shoved them at her.

Lauren shuffled the birth certificate to the bottom of the sheaf and stared. She flipped to the next page and swallowed.

"Something bad?" Jesse asked.

That depended. Jesse would probably say good right now. "It's a will Shelley's mother did online." Lauren struggled for the breath to continue. "It leaves all of her property to Shelley and names you as Shelley's father and guardian."

"Let me see." Jesse sat back next to her, shoulder to shoulder, hip to knee.

A pulse throbbed in her throat.

"She's mine. I knew she was." His voice was barely a whisper, as if he were in awe. "Woo-hoo!" he shouted.

His abrupt change made her start.

He threw his arms around her in a hug.

Lauren gave herself a moment to enjoy the feel, the memories of Jesse's arms around her, before she disentangled. "Jesse, even with the will, the probate court will have to approve the guardianship."

"So, what do I have to do, get a DNA test to prove I'm her biological father?"

"Basically, and show you can take care of her. If we work through DSS, we can get their support. You can ease into a relationship with Shelley."

"And she'd have to go into foster care while we do. No. I've known more than a few people who've been foster kids and can't say any of them had fond memories of it."

Jesse took her hand, and a shot of warmth ran through her. It would be so easy to give into him. But, what if Shelley turned out not to be his daughter and he didn't want her then? Lauren had been a college student when her father had left her mother and essentially cut off contact with Lauren. The hurt was still there. Shelley was a toddler who'd already lost her mother and her aunt. Lauren's mind went into overtime for an argument Jesse might be open to. *Money.* He'd always been a saver and a planner for the future when he was finished racing. He was finished now and appeared strapped financially.

"DNA testing is expensive. If you work through DSS, there's only a small fee."

A muscle worked in his jaw. "Despite appearances the other morning and the fact that most of my investments went to help Dad pay Mom's medical expenses, I have some left I could sell."

"Jesse-Daddy house stinky," Shelley interrupted.

Jesse had Lauren so absorbed in him and trying to make her point, she hadn't noticed Mom and Shelley had returned.

"It needs airing out, and isn't in as good a shape as I'd hoped." His voice was flat.

"You'd need to show you can care properly for her," Lauren repeated, steeling herself for Jesse's resistance again.

His shoulders slumped, draining the steel from her.

"What's this about?" her mother asked.

Jesse spoke before she could. "Crystal, Shelley's mother, had a will naming me Shelley's guardian, and as her father, which I guess I need to prove to the court."

When he glanced at her, Lauren nodded.

Her mother sat between them, and Shelley climbed up on his lap. She reached over and touched Lauren's cheek. "Pretty."

Lauren wrestled with the sensation flowing through her and memories of a long-ago conversation with Jesse about how many kids they'd wanted.

"You and Shelley need a better place to live until you can improve the cottage," her mother said. "My side of the duplex has three bedrooms, plenty of room for you."

Lauren swallowed the lump in her throat. Jesse living right next door to her.

"I'd pay rent," he said.

Her mother waved him off. "We can work that out in our other agreement. You'll need daycare."

"One of the reasons behind my suggestion," Lauren interjected to get a place in the conversation.

Her mother looked at her for an explanation.

"She wants to get DSS involved," Jesse beat her to it.

"We don't need to do that," her mother said, joining Jesse in shutting her out.

"Dad," he said. "I planned to talk him into moving here eventually anyway. This should clinch his decision. I can't think of anyone I would rather have watching my daughter."

"Perfect," her mother said.

Heads together, Jesse and her mother discussed their plan.

Lauren crossed and uncrossed her ankles. "Since you've chosen not to take my legal advice … She closed and opened her eyes. Did she sound as priggish to him as she did to herself? Lauren softened her tone. "You may want to have Ray or Gerry handle Crystal's will. Or another law firm."

Jesse's head shot up.

That had gotten his attention. Lauren scratched at a nick in one of her otherwise perfectly manicured fingernails. What a case she was. Jealous—that was the only word she could come up with—jealous of Jesse's attention to her mother and Shelley.

"No, I want you," he said.

Lauren dismissed the fanciful connotations his words conjured in her. He was talking about a business relationship.

"You'll represent us? Shelley and me?"

Three sets of eyes gazed at her in expectation, two sets that were so alike with amber flecks and long lashes. It went against every ounce of better judgment she had, but what else could she say?

"Yes, I will."

What have I done? she asked herself for at least the tenth time since she'd returned to her office. Her plan this morning had been to lure Jesse into leaving town with the deal for the Morrison property, Jesse's property, that Ray had told her about this morning. She tucked a hair that had strayed from her French braid behind her ear and tried to focus on the documents in front of her. Was that only this morning?

The ring of the office phone cut short her attempt to get back to work. Maybe Jesse had had second thoughts.

"Lauren, can *we* see you in my office," Ray said in an almost replay of earlier.

She replaced the receiver. The Jesse she'd know rarely had second thoughts. Except about her. She swallowed. Just like that the insecure twenty-year-old college student whose father had just left replaced the competent professional woman she'd become. *Dad had said I'd always be his girl. Jesse had said he'd wait for me forever.* Lauren shook off her ridiculous sentimental thoughts and went to see what Ray wanted.

"What is this?" he demanded before she'd even gotten all the way into his office. He and Gerry were looking at the computer screen.

Perversely, she took her time crossing the room so she could see. "New business," she said, focusing on the folder she'd added in Jesse's computer records for the probate of Crystal's will.

"Didn't you tell him about Ken's offer?"

Lauren didn't know what the offer had to do with the will. "I did. He's already made a gentleman's agreement with someone else." Although, Ray and Gerry would find out soon enough, she wasn't going to share now that the agreement was with her mother. "Nothing is finalized yet."

"Let us know if the deal is or isn't finalized," Gerry said.

"Yeah," Ray agreed. "Better yet, talk him out of it."

"Ken isn't happy about the development," Gerry said.

His older brother gave him the evil eye. *Geez.* Ken was the firm's biggest client, but from Gerry's comment, you'd think he was their only client. The burger and fries she'd grabbed on her way back after leaving Jesse and her mom still discussing details sat heavy in her stomach. She and Brittany hadn't had much work lately. Ray and Gerrie handled all of Ken's work.

"And the kid, custody thing. How quickly can you wrap that up?" Ray asked.

"Mr. Brewster is anxious to finalize his guardianship as quickly as possible. Probate of the will will take the usual time."

"Yeah, but Brewster doesn't have to stick around here for that part. I mean, he doesn't seem like a person who'd be happy in a place like Indigo Bay. I'm sure he's anxious to get back to his business concerns in California."

"Let me know if you have any trouble getting Brewster's guardianship hearing expedited," Gerry added. "I can talk to the Family Court judge."

Lauren bristled at what she took to be an insinuation that she'd need his help to pull strings, that she would pull strings. "I can handle it."

"Fine. Do it." Ray dismissed her.

Lauren tamped down the urge to stomp back to her office. If Jesse decided to renovate the mansion with her mother, he'd be here months or longer. Much longer if he and his father opened a custom bike shop here. She dropped into her desk chair and opened the filing she'd started for Family Court. The contrariness that had sprouted with her bosses' comments and attitude had her inclined to take her time on it.

She knew why *she* wanted Jesse's time in Indigo Bay as short as possible. She'd admit she wasn't as immune to Jesse's charms as she'd like to be. But their past had proven to her, at least, that they wouldn't work together as a couple. And she'd be a lot more immune to him if he were 2,000 miles away again.

Lauren stared at the computer screen. What she couldn't put her finger on was why Ray and Gerry were so anxious to get Jesse out of town.

CHAPTER 5

Jesse sat out on the bench again, head in hands, working out the call to his father in his head. He'd driven Sonja and Shelley and her things to Sonja's place, and come back to get his bike and pack up what few things of his he'd taken into the cottage yesterday. He'd disappointed his father over the years, particularly by not finishing the engineering degree he'd started out of high school. The degree Dad had said would give him a career to fall back on after his racing career ended. Jesse rotated his bad ankle. Dad had always said Jesse could do better than him, better than running a bike shop. But what was wrong with that? Mom and Dad had been happy and, as far as he could tell, comfortable enough until Mom's medical bills piled up. And Jesse couldn't have asked for a better childhood, better parents. They'd always been there for him.

He breathed in the salty breeze off the ocean. Dad wouldn't be disappointed about Shelley. *Well, maybe about my careless behavior and the circumstances of her birth.* He should go ahead and make the call and get back to his daughter. Shelley was his responsibility, not Sonja's.

She'd been more than generous, much more so than Lauren. If he knew Lauren, which was up in the air, she'd only been doing her legal duty to protect him if Shelley wasn't his. But she was. The little girl was what he and Lauren could have had if he hadn't screwed up.

Jesse punched his dad's number before he headed back down the road of regrets he'd finally been able to steer away from.

"Hi, son," his father answered.

"Hey, Dad, how's it going?"

"All right, better if I had more to do."

His lungs burned at the resignation in his father's voice. Dad had put in long hours at the shop, and Mom had been Dad's best friend. Like Lauren had once been his. Any free time Dad had had, he'd spent cruising the coast on his bike with Mom. "I have a remedy for that. I could use your help here."

Jesse stood and paced in front of the bench as he told his dad about running into Lauren here, although not the circumstances other than her working at the law firm handing Uncle Jim's estate, and about the mansion, his agreement with Sonja to renovate it, and his plans for opening a bike shop. He saved Shelley for last.

"I have a granddaughter? Shelley." Dad's voice was think with wonder. "So that's what the woman had for you."

Jesse's own throat constructed. "Yeah. Shelley looks just like those pictures Mom had of herself and Grandma and Grandpa when she was small. But what do you mean, the woman had for me?

"I got a phone call forwarded from the old house number from a woman who said you'd left something at her place that she wanted to return."

That was one way to put it.

"I said she could send it to you care of the Indigo Bay Post Office. Thought that was safe enough. When do I get to meet little Shelley?" his father asked.

"About that. I have a huge favor to ask. I need someone to help take care of Shelley while I'm working."

"You want me to come?"

Jesse held his breath.

"Give me a few days to get my stuff here in storage and sublease the condo. The association has a waiting list of people who want places here. Then, I'll need a week to drive there."

"By yourself?"

"You did," his father shot back. "Your old man isn't *that* old."

True, Dad was only in his early fifties, He'd just seemed to grow so much older with Mom's illness and death.

"I'll let you know when I have everything together to leave."

Jesse couldn't remember the last time his father had been this enthused—at all enthused—about anything. "Thanks, Dad. I really appreciate this."

"A little Shelley. Huh. Looks like your mom," his father mused. "I'll call you in a few days."

Jesse's phone flashed *call ended*. He whistled as he walked to his truck. He might not have as much difficulty getting Dad to come in on the bike shop here as he'd thought. Assuming he wanted to stay here after the mansion renovations were done. He put the truck in gear. Oddly, something about Indigo Bay— something other than Lauren being here—made it feel like home, even though he'd only been in town a couple days. And, he wouldn't lie to himself. The challenge of making Lauren change her mind about him hanging around had a certain attraction. Not that he was looking to revive their former relationship. But they could be friends.

Two cars were already in the driveway of Sonja's duplex when he pulled up. Hers, from the magnet sign for Kostner Real Estate on the passenger door, and Lauren's. His heart rate ticked up. Maybe Sonja's offer wasn't as great an idea as he'd thought. If Lauren didn't want to have anything to do with him, as her recommendation he have Ray or Gerry handle Crystal's estate indicated, living right next door, seeing her all the time could be uncomfortable. Jesse rubbed the back of his neck. He'd better start the renovations on the cottage, to give him and Dad and Shelley somewhere to live. He took his time parking the pickup and bike trailer in front of the house and getting out.

His life had been so simple three days ago when he'd breezed into town, inheritance in mind, ready to make a new start for himself in what had appeared from his research and first impression to be an idyllic resort town. What more could a guy want? Beautiful beaches, warm weather, traffic-free stretches of windy roads for riding, no connections, no commitments. That was before he'd run into Lauren. Before her mother had become his new best friend and business partner. Before Shelley had been dropped on him.

Ignoring the twinge in his bad ankle, he bounded up the front steps to Sonja's side of the house. He hadn't felt this alive since before his accident. The day before his accident when he'd bought a surprise engagement ring for Lauren. A ring he still had. Now it might be an investment in a different future. He could sell it to pay for DNA testing if he needed to.

"Hush, Xena," Lauren said giving the large black dog fidgeting beside her a pet on the head. She opened her front door a crack so Xena couldn't get out and glanced toward the other side of the house. Then, reassuring Xena that she would return, Lauren slipped out and into her car. At the end of the driveway, she took a moment to admire the brilliant orange and red sun over the beach to the east. Jesse's truck was gone. But the bike trailer was still on the street where he'd parked it last night. She'd heard him pull up and had peeked out her window. He must be at the beach doing his community service. What had she expected? To wake up and have it all be a bad dream?

She couldn't help but wonder if Jesse might not be waking up to the same thought. The walls of the duplex weren't very thick, and she'd woken several times during the night to Shelley crying out and Xena whimpering and nudging her with her nose to do something. The low murmur of Jesse consoling the little girl had followed. Lauren's heart went out to them both. All the more reason to maintain her distance from father and daughter, which wasn't going to be easy with them right next door.

She swung by Sweet Caroline's for a cinnamon roll and coffee for her breakfast and bought a half dozen rolls to take into the office for Brittany and the guys and any clients scheduled for today. Not that she had any coming in. She sighed. She could always have the leftovers for lunch. The waistband of her skirt seemed to tighten at the thought. Not the best idea, like many of her recent ideas. At the office, Lauren juggled her briefcase, coffee, and the rolls so she could unlock the front door. The key wouldn't turn.

"Good morning."

Lauren dropped the bag of cinnamon rolls at Brittany's unexpected greeting.

"Having trouble with your new key?" Brittany asked.

New key? What new key? "Yeah," she fudged.

"Let me see if mine works."

Lauren stepped aside and Brittany unlocked the door.

"There we go," Brittany said.

Lauren searched her co-worker's face for any sign of smugness that she knew Lauren didn't have a key to the new lock their bosses must have had installed without her knowledge. She didn't see any. Of course, she didn't see any, she chided herself. Brittany wasn't conspiring against her. Ray and Gerry weren't conspiring against her. Jesse hadn't appeared in Indigo Bay planning to set up a partnership with her mother. He hadn't come looking for Lauren, as much as an ever-growing kernel inside her might wish that. Him, her, here. It was all coincidence. She followed Brittany inside.

Brittany dropped her bag on her desk. "Are those cinnamon rolls to share, or do you have an early morning meeting?"

"Totally to share." Lauren placed the bag on the front desk and opened it for Brittany, releasing a warm cinnamon scent.

Brittany pulled out one of the gooey confections. "Mmmm." She looked up. "I think we have some more takers.

Lauren followed Brittany's gaze to the door, which Jesse was opening to let Shelley toddle in ahead of him.

"I assume he's here to meet with you, although I wouldn't mind being closed in an office alone with him." Brittany's gaze dropped to Shelley. "Fill me in after your meeting."

"The records are all on the network," Lauren said with an animosity that had come out of nowhere." She pasted a smile on her face. Not out of nowhere. Out of jealousy. She'd deal with that later.

"Good morning ladies." Jesse's cheery smile looked as fake as hers and contrasted with the circles under his eyes. "Do you have a few minutes, Lauren?"

"I do, come into my office," she said all business.

"I'll watch your daughter," Brittany said, her voice rising in question, nodding at Shelley who stood with one arm around Jesse's leg and her other thumb firmly in her mouth.

"No," Lauren and Jesse said in unison.

How did Brittany know Shelley was his daughter? Lauren relaxed her tensed muscles. She didn't. She just assumed as any normal person might.

He picked up Shelley, who kept her thumb planted where it was. "She's been through a lot, meeting a lot of strangers the past few days."

"I understand," Brittany said. "Moving here and all. Don't forget your rolls." She handed Lauren the bag as she started to lead Jesse to her office.

"From Caroline's?" he asked.

"Yes." Lauren took the bag.

"Your mother made us eggs this morning, but I'm sure we could down a cinnamon roll or two."

They must have all been up at the crack of dawn for them to have eaten a cooked breakfast before he'd left for his community service job. He would have never had time afterwards and gotten here so close on her heels. Lauren scanned Jesse's tired face. *Or earlier.*

"Could we sit on the couch?" Jesse asked as she led them into her office and headed toward her desk.

"If you'd be more comfortable." She'd be more comfortable with her desk between them, preventing any chance of Jesse or Shelley touching her and chipping at her attorney-client wall that her pesky emotions kept trying to break through from the other side.

Jesse dropped onto the couch with Shelley on his lap. Lauren sat at the other end, positioning herself knees toward Jesse so she could face him. The Sweet Caroline's bag between them. She swallowed a sip of her coffee. "Help yourself."

"This could get messy." He nodded at Shelly.

"The couch only looks like leather." Whereas Ray and Gerry's furniture *was* leather. "It can be wiped off. So what can I do for you this morning?"

What she recognized as mischief flashed in his eyes, and her cheeks warmed at the possibilities her general question opened.

"Donut, Jesse-Daddy." Shelley interrupted before he could answer. She reached in the bag.

"Better than donuts." Jesse helped his daughter lift out a roll and wrapped a napkin from the bag around it. He took one for himself and offered Lauren one.

Her stomach grumbled.

"I'll take that for a yes." He passed her the bag.

Lauren focused her complete attention on the cinnamon rolls while her reheated cheeks cooled. She'd long ago mastered the propensity to blush that went with her fair skin and blond hair. Except where Jesse was concerned.

"Aside from whatever made you blush the first time …"

She crumpled the bag closed and placed it on the table in front of the couch.

"I called yesterday and got an appointment at the DNA testing center in Charleston this morning. You said something about a form that has to be filed."

"You got an appointment that quickly?"

He scuffed his boot against the rug. "You know it's not my style, but the woman scheduling the appointment recognized my name. She was a fan. I kind of played the motocross champion card. She squeezed me in." He buried his face in his daughter's hair. "Speed is important here. More important than in any race I drove. I have to secure Shelley's place with me."

Jesse's words kicked a hole in her already shaky wall. "I heard you up with her last night. Through the wall of my room. Reassuring her."

"Sorry. For all the good I did. She kept waking up anyway."

Lauren touched the arm he had around Shelley. "She's been through so much. You got her back to sleep. She wasn't up crying continuously. I can vouch for your consoling skills."

Their gazes locked. Why had she said that?

"When people let me," he said, reminding her of how he'd tried when her father had left, and she'd pushed him away.

Like he'd pushed her away after his accident. Lauren cemented a few bricks back into her wall. "Back to your reason for stopping in. The form is for me to file for you once you have your results. You don't need it today. All you need to do is authorize the results to come to Acer and Acer, or give me a copy when you have them."

"We can get going, then." Jesse stood, breaking the remnant of the emotional connection she'd already nicked.

"Wait. Is Mom watching Shelly for you while you go to your appointment?" She wasn't ready to let him leave, and it was a reasonable question, although not directly related to their attorney-client relationship.

"No, she's gone into work. She has showings this morning. She offered to reschedule them, but I couldn't ask her to do that."

"Gamma's gone. Mommy's gone. Aunt Tara's gone."

With a look of sadness no child that small should feel, Shelley gripped Jesse so fiercely it squeezed Lauren's heart. "Gramma will be back after work." Had she really just referred to her mother as Shelley's grandmother. Professionally, she knew better. It had just slipped out.

"Gamma work?" Shelley gazed up at Jesse.

"Yes, we'll see Gramma later."

She should discourage Jesse and her mother and the grandmother thing. Shelley was going to be confused and hurt when Jesse and the little girl left Indigo Bay after the guardianship was finalized and the mansion renovations done. If he stayed for the renovations. The Acers and Ken Kostner might still entice him to sell. Or when Jesse left on his own if it turned out he wasn't Shelley's father, as he'd left Lauren despite his professed love.

Shelley nodded, "`Ren later?"

"I don't know. We'll have to wait and see."

Jesse was right in discouraging Shelley from attaching to her, too. Falling for the little girl would be easy and dangerous to Lauren's equilibrium, since Jesse would be part of the package. She should be thankful for his discouragement. So where was the resentment and feeling of being left out coming from?

"No, `Ren. Gamma later." Shelley burst into tears.

"It's okay." Jesse patted her on the back, his expression saying it was anything but okay.

"Maybe you should reschedule your appointment when Mom can watch Shelley."

Jesse's face hardened. "She's so tired, she'll fall asleep in the car. Besides, I need to be able to handle whatever."

"It's okay to accept help."

The way Jesse worked his jaw, Lauren knew she'd said the wrong thing. She was the one who'd turned down Jesse's and everyone else's help in the past to prove she was strong enough to handle her life herself. She was, and strong enough to help Jesse as well.

"I'll come along and stay with Shelley while you go in for your appointment? In a professional capacity. As your attorney."

The grin of thanks Jesse shot her said he believed the last part about as much as she did.

CHAPTER 6

"Lauren?" A tap on his shoulder woke Jesse from a dream of him and Lauren laying on the beach, his beach, looking up at the stars.

"No `Ren," a childish voice said.

He lifted his head from his laptop where he'd fallen asleep working on the mansion renovation drawing and blinked to see his daughter standing next to the desk. He swallowed the bitter tang in his mouth. Some parent he was. He'd been so out, he hadn't heard Shelley get up from her second nap of the day. She could have been into anything, and he would have had no idea.

"No Gamma," Shelley said.

He tapped the spacebar and glanced at the time. Two. They'd gotten back to Sonja's duplex about 12:30 with Shelley fast asleep. He'd worked on the drawing for at least forty-five minutes, so he hadn't been asleep long.

"Gramma's still at work," he said. The black expression that crossed Lauren's face every time Shelley said Gamma, flashed in his mind. He probably shouldn't encourage Shelley to call Sonja Gramma, even though Sonja was fine with it.

"Hungy," Shelley said.

"I'll bet you are. Me, too. Let's see what we can rummage up." He stood and lifted Shelley into his arms and carried her into the kitchen.

They'd both missed lunch. Shelley had fallen asleep in the car on the way to Charleston, probably from the bla-bla lullaby of polite-strangers conversation between him and Lauren. When Lauren had offered to stay with Shelley in the car while he went in the testing center for his appointment so his daughter could sleep, he'd gotten a glimpse of the girl, woman, who'd captured and once held his heart. The only women who ever really had. Lauren had shuttered that glimpse when he'd come back out from his appointment, and she'd brought up Ken's offer to buy the mansion again.

Jesse pulled open a cupboard. That had started a livelier conversation in which Jesse did his best to impress Lauren with his plans for the mansion. He had no idea if he'd made any headway, but they'd woken up Shelley, who'd started crying. Lauren had calmed the little girl with a repertoire of children's songs, becoming his old Lauren again.

"How about a peanut butter and jelly sandwich?"

Shelley shook her head. "No p'butter."

The emphatic way she said no made him wonder if she was allergic to peanuts. Weren't a lot of kids now? He jammed his fingers through his hair. There was so much he didn't know. But Dad would be here soon to help. Together they'd figure things out. But that wasn't the partnership he truly wanted. He wanted Lauren. But he couldn't have that until he proved to her and himself that he wasn't a screw-up, that he could succeed at something other than racing.

"Cereal." Shelley pointed at the box in the cupboard.

For lunch?

She smiled up at him.

Why not? He grabbed the box, put it on the table, and sat Shelley in the booster seat that for whatever reason Sonja had had tucked away in a closet. Then he'd grabbed two bowls and the milk and made them each a bowlful.

"'Poon," Shelley said.

"You're right, we need spoons. He got them, sat and dug into his cereal, warming when Shelley mimicked him.

"What do we have here?" Sonja walked in the kitchen door to a shout of "Gamma" from Shelley.

"A late lunch." Jesse scuffed his boot on the vinyl floor. "How did your showings go?"

"One sale, and one like to see more. How about your appointment?"

He shrugged. "Good. Lauren came with us."

Sonja raised an eyebrow.

"As my attorney," he added.

"Of course. Has someone had her n-a-p?"

"Two. One in the car and one when we got home."

"It's a beautiful day. Would you mind if I took her to the public beach? There's a playground there. Maybe I can tire her out so she'll sleep better tonight."

Shelley was his responsibility. He should be the one taking her to the playground. But Sonja looked like her offer was something she wanted to do.

"Okay, and as thanks, I'll pick up some steaks and grill them for us."

"Include Lauren. I don't know how well she eats sometimes."

"Yeah, I owe her, too. Shelley fell asleep on our way to the testing center. Lauren stayed in the car with her while I went in for my appointment."

Sonja waved him off. "You don't owe either of us anything. Lauren wouldn't have gone with you and Shelley if she didn't want to."

Was she telling him Lauren wanted to be with him? Lauren and her mother were close. She might know something like that.

"And no need to go out for steaks. I have some in the freezer."

"Hmmm?" He was still back on the possibility that Lauren might want to be with him.

"Use the steaks in the freezer. That will give you more time to work on those plans we talked about."

The plans he'd fallen asleep over earlier. "Right."

"And would you show Lauren your plans? She seems to think I'm getting myself in over my head with our project. Maybe if she sees things spelled out more clearly in a drawing, she'll understand this isn't some pie-in-the-sky dream I've come up with."

"Sure thing."

From their discussions, Jesse thought Sonja knew exactly what she wanted and what she was getting herself into. It was him who was in over his head. Jesse glanced at his daughter and thought about Lauren singing to her in the car. His dangerous waters had nothing to do with the renovation project. But, even with his battered, closed-down heart, he was a strong swimmer, a Southern California surfer. There wasn't a wave he couldn't conquer, not even the tidal wave Lauren had become.

Lauren left the county building, fuming the whole drive home. Gerry couldn't have given her the deed for one of Ken's acquisitions to file before he and Ray had left for their four-hour lunch or wherever they'd been, so she might have had real work to do this afternoon. No, he had to saunter in at twenty of five and ask her to rush over and do it before the county offices closed at five. And with the documents to file, he'd handed her the key to the new front door lock he'd allegedly "forgotten" to give her before she'd left yesterday.

She slammed her brakes as she belatedly noticed the traffic light in front of her, one of the few in Indigo Bay, turning red. The car screeched to a halt. She couldn't rid herself of the thought that somehow Ray and Gerry were punishing her for not convincing Jesse to sell his property. Why did she put up with it anyway? The light turned green. *Easy.* To make partner, for the chance to take over the practice when the brothers retired. To achieve her dream and security—except the lack of new business, other than Jesse's had her questioning the security part.

Her mother's car wasn't in the driveway when she pulled in, only Jesse's truck minus the bike trailer. He wouldn't be out on the bike with Shelley, would he? She stepped out of the car. Just because she didn't see the trailer didn't mean he was out on his bike or that he had Shelley out with him. Mom could have taken her somewhere. Nor was any of this her business. Except that it was her business if she was representing Jesse and his petition to be confirmed as Shelley's guardian. Not everyone thought a two-year-old belonged on a motorcycle. She'd talk with him about that later. Right now, a glass of wine sounded like an excellent idea to her.

When she walked into her kitchen, the aroma of sizzling beef accosted her hunger through the screened window above the sink. Mom must have Jesse grilling for her. That had been Lauren's job since her parents split. She opened the refrigerator, took out the wine, and looked at the leftover frozen mac and cheese she'd planned to have for supper. After pouring her wine, she stuck the plate of mac and cheese in the microwave. Before she could push start, a knock sounded at the door.

Jesse smiled at her through the window in the door.

"Hey," she said, her heart pounding as opened it. Pounding not because of the smile. Not because it was him, looking so Jesse in a tight white t-shirt worn almost transparent, a motocross rider and *Do It in the Dirt* emblazed across his chest. *No.* Pounding because he'd startled her. Nothing more than that.

"Hey, yourself. Your mother told me to invite you over for supper. I'm grilling steaks."

"Yeah, I smelled them through the window." That was what was drawing her to him. A medium rare steak would beat her mac and cheese by a mile.

"I've got potatoes and corn on the cob on the grill, too," he added as if she needed any more convincing.

"And there's stuff in your mother's fridge if you want to put together a salad."

"Sounds good." She could do supper with Jesse, as long as she had her mother and Shelley as a safety buffer. "So, did Mom run out for something?"

"She took Shelley down to the beach to the playground."

"Then, I expect they'll be back soon. I'll go over and make that salad."

Jesse avoided her gaze. "She called a couple of minutes ago. They ran into a friend of your mother's who was at the playground with her granddaughter. The four of them are going to get something to eat on the Boardwalk."

"Oh. Then it's just …"

"You and me babe," he finished for her. "And I'm okay without the salad."

She wasn't okay with any of it now. In fact, the leftover mac and cheese, eating alone, was sounding better and better.

"This isn't a setup, is it? You. Me. Supper."

Jesse raised his hands in surrender. "No. I offered to grill steaks for your mother as thanks for taking Shelley to the playground so I could get in some work drawing the renovation plans. It was your mother's idea to include you. I am totally innocent."

Lauren's initial embarrassment at accusing Jesse of trying to get her alone turned into irritation at her mother. Supper could still be a setup. Just on her mother's part, not Jesse's.

"I have to get back to the grill," he said.

At the mention of the grill, Lauren picked up the scent of the cooking meat again. Truthfully, the mac and cheese didn't sound at all appetizing. And neither did eating alone. She was a big girl. She could have a dinner with Jesse without succumbing to his charms. They could sit kitty corner on opposite sides of the picnic table, so he'd have room to stretch his legs without touching her. *Yeah.* She could do it.

"I'll change my clothes, make that salad, and meet you out back."

"See you in a few."

Lauren closed the door behind him and took a gulp of wine. Jesse was rarely, if ever innocent when it came to pursuing something he wanted. But what, exactly was he pursuing? He wasn't exuding any particular charm. So despite all of *her* errant thoughts, it didn't look like it was her he was pursuing.

Upstairs in her room, she rejected a cute pair of shorts she'd picked up last week for a worn pair of denim capris and pulled on a baggy garnet t-shirt with *University of South Carolina* in black across the front that she had left over from law school. Her armor of least attractive clothes offered some defense. But the less time alone with Jesse, the better. She'd head over to her mother's kitchen by way of the front doors and take her time making the salad. To add a little more time to the process, Lauren stopped in her kitchen on her way and polished off the rest of her glass of wine before thinking that getting tipsy wasn't any way to build her resolve against Jesse. His smile. That smile. The one she'd always thought of as hers flashed in front of her eyes.

Lauren refilled her wine glass before letting herself out her front door.

~

Aside from Lauren giving him a wide berth that had him wondering if he should have showered before supper, their meal together went off okay. If okay meant reminiscent of dining with a maiden aunt who wanted to catch up on what you'd been doing but was hesitant to ask any questions that might give her real answers. Jesse held the door open so Lauren could carry her share of the dishes and food into her mother's place ahead of him. What had he expected? Them to fall right back into couple speak? And it wasn't as if he'd been any better. He'd kept his side of the conversation every bit as impersonal.

Lauren placed the food and dishes on the counter and opened the dishwasher.

"Leave the dishes. I'll do them later. Your mom wanted me to show you her, our, ideas for the B&B renovations." There he went again. *He* wanted to show her to show her the designs he'd done online. "They're on my laptop in the other room."

"It's no problem." Lauren started loading the dishwasher.

Didn't she want to see the plans? Or was it the laptop being in his room? "I'll go get the laptop. We can look at them at the table."

He strode from the kitchen, grabbed his computer, and made it back halfway across the living room when his foot gave way, sending him and the computer into a face planter with the thinly carpeted hardwood floor. Only a quick twist as the floor came up fast saved the computer and his face from the impact. The same couldn't be said about his shoulder. Jesse rolled to his back with a groan, closed his eyes, and placed the laptop on his stomach.

Lauren's footsteps reverberated faintly on the floor. "Are you all right?"

He opened his eyes to Lauren's face inches from his and stared at the intensity of the concern on her perfect, to him—and he'd challenge anyone who said otherwise—features.

She smoothed his hair, lighting a fire that made him think twice before moving the laptop off him and onto the floor.

"I heard you fall. Can you get up?" she asked.

He studied her earnest expression and knew what he had to do. "Maybe you could help me." He offered her his hand. He had to know.

She took it, and he pulled her from her knees onto his chest, cupping her face in his palms. Jesse stared up at her. *So beautiful.* He pressed his lips to hers, hesitating when she stiffened and deepening the kiss when she relaxed and returned it.

Through the haze of bliss, he heard a noise. A door closing. "I think your mother's home."

"Mmmm." Lauren kissed him quiet, but only for a second.

"Your mother. Shelley. Here," he murmured against her pliant lips.

Lauren was up on her knees beside him so fast he'd swear her movement had caused a whoosh of cold air between them.

"What do we have here?" Sonja asked.

Now Lauren was on her feet. "Jesse fell."

He leaned up on one elbow, unfortunately the one he'd landed on in the fall. He winced. "My foot goes out sometimes. The accident." He didn't know whether the embarrassment heating him was from the suspicion that Sonja had seen them before Lauren had moved away or from admitting his weakness. It didn't matter. Both his foot and Lauren were weaknesses.

"Jesse-Daddy boo boo?"

He'd forgotten all about Shelley, like when he'd fallen asleep. "I'm okay, sweetie." *Well*, except for his ego. He rolled to a sitting position and used his good foot to stand.

"Can you walk?" Lauren asked.

"Yes," he said too sharply, testing his other leg to make sure he wasn't lying. "Uh, could you get the laptop?"

"Sure." She bent to pick it up from the floor.

While Lauren wasn't looking, Jesse took one long stride to reach a side chair so he could hold the back for support. Just in case. From there it was only two long steps to the kitchen doorway.

"Me help, Jesse-Daddy." Shelley took his free hand.

He glanced down at the little girl, his heart filling with a love different from any he'd experienced before. "Thank you. You'll be a big help." A bead of sweat ran down his spine as he recalculated the number of steps to the doorway, increasing it from two to four for Shelley's shorter stride. He'd have to put his weight on his bad foot, the foot closest to Shelly twice, rather than once.

Lauren smiled at them as if waiting for him to go ahead.

"You can take the laptop into the kitchen. Shelley and I have this."

"You sure?" Lauren asked, concern lacing her face.

"I'm sure." He got out through gritted teeth. He didn't want the feeling their kiss had ignited in both of them to turn to pity on her part.

"All right."

"Come on." Sonja looped her arm through Lauren's, eying the laptop. "You were going to look at the plans Jesse and I have for the B&B?"

Jesse waited a moment until they'd reached the doorway and tested his weight on his bad leg. No weakness. "Let's go."

"Go," Shelley repeated.

The four steps to the doorway he'd estimated turned into five. Shelley was a bitty little thing. Another couple steps got them to the chair at the table, where either Lauren or Sonja had the laptop open and booting. He bent and hugged Shelley, breathing in what he could only describe as her little girl scent. "You were a big help." He slipped into the chair.

Shelley scrambled up on his lap, stepping on his bad foot.

I won't wince. I won't wince. He didn't want Lauren thinking he'd really needed any help walking from the other room. Jesse released a whoosh when the pain subsided.

"'Puter on." Shelley bounced on his lap and pointed at the spinning start-up screen that was still running.

"In a minute." He looked up at Lauren. "It's older, sometimes takes a while to boot."

Swift. Why had he said that? To underscore his bad financial situation? As if she didn't already have a good enough idea of it.

"Why don't you sit with Jesse? I'll take Shelly up for her bath," Sonja said.

"Bath. Bubbles?" Shelley lifted her arms to Lauren's mother.

"We bought bubble bath while we were out."

The loss of warmth Jesse felt when Sonja lifted Shelley from his lap was replaced by a radiance of heat when Lauren sat in the chair next to him and scooted closer to look at the screen. He clicked the icon to load his CAD program.

"This will just take another minute." Or several minutes, depending on how the computer felt. He held his breath. Sometimes, it didn't load at all the first try. He didn't need more signs of his come-down in life reapplying any of the loser patina their kiss may have— *no had*—removed. He didn't have any reason to think it hadn't. Lauren hadn't had any complaints in the physical romance department in the past, and the injury to his leg wouldn't have affected any expertise he'd had in that area.

Yes! The program window popped right open to the B&B plans. "This is the basic layout of the structure," he said, clicking on the mansion's formal entryway to show a picture of what it looked like now—Sonja had had photos from the real estate listing—and how Sonja envisioned it looking when the work was finished.

Lauren leaned closer, her breath soft on his cheek as she leaned in.

"You can do this?" she asked, interrupting Jesse's brain path into softness, the softness of Lauren's hair draped over him, of her cheek, of her lips beneath his.

"Yeah, it was one of the engineering courses I took." That should get him a point too, finishing a class, using what he'd learned. Lauren had reassured him more than once in the past that she didn't care whether he had a college degree or not, but he'd never fully believed her.

"No, I meant the physical labor." Her gaze dropped to his foot. "I assume it, what happened earlier when you fell, is from your racing accident. Does it bother you often?"

Jesse cracked his knuckles. So much for impressing Lauren with his design skills, with having completed at least part of his engineering degree. "Mainly when I'm tired." *And the physical discomfort doesn't bother me nearly as much as not being able to race, to finish my racing career.* "I usually know my limit, but I've had a lot of unexpected things going on the past couple days. I'll hire out what I need to hire out." He wished he could take back the defensiveness in his last statement, but he was defensive.

Lauren went back to studying the computer screen. "Mom's put a lot more thought into the project than I knew."

Mom, not him. *Brewster, get a grip. It isn't some kind of contest.* But it was.

"Want me to email you a copy of the plans? I can put them in a PDF." Was that supposed to dazzle her, too? He was a sick case.

"No, I'll have Mom print a copy for me."

He clicked the program closed. "I should be getting Shelley to bed."

She pushed her chair away from the table, from him and stood. "Right." She moved her weight from foot to foot. "Do you need help upstairs?"

"No, I've got it." *Even if I have to crawl up on my hands and knees.*

"Okay. See you around. I'll be looking for your DNA results at the office."

That was it? Jesse rose and placed one foot close enough to hers to make her stepping away more difficult without appearing to block her. He lowered his head and lightly brushed her lips with his before stepping back.

Lauren blinked twice as if she was unsure what had happened before turning to flee out the kitchen door.

Jesse watched the door close behind her. The importance of the project's success had ratcheted up a notch. He wouldn't be free to get on with his life until he'd proven to Lauren, as well as himself, that he wasn't a washed-up failure in the race of life—whether or not that proof got him anywhere relationship-wise with her.

CHAPTER 7

Aman was sitting on her porch. A very large man. Lauren had her directional on, but hesitated to pull into the driveway. Since it was such a nice day, she'd decided to swing by home for lunch and let the dog out in the fenced backyard for the afternoon. But she didn't have to. Xena often stayed in for most of the day. She could just drive by and back to the office.

Then, the truck and trailer on the other side of the street caught her eye. California plates. Jesse's dad? But Jesse didn't expect him for another week or so. At least he hadn't the last she'd known. It hadn't been easy, but over the weekend, since the toe-curling kiss that she'd blocked from her mind, most of the time, she'd managed to steer clear of any contact with Jesse. His dad's plans could have changed.

She pulled in, wiped her hands on her skirt, grabbed her house key, threw open the car door, and stepped out.

"Hello, I'm Jeff Brewster, Jesse's dad." The man had stood while she'd parked the car. "You must be Lauren. I recognize you from pictures he showed me."

Jesse showed his family, his dad, pictures of her? That shouldn't surprise her. They'd been pretty serious for a while. Fingering the key in her hand turned the lock to the memory of their kiss, the feel of his solid chest, his strong arms around her. *Get a grip on yourself.* The other night didn't mean anything in the larger scheme of things. She and Jesse were still the same people, people with different outlooks on life, not really any different than when she'd fallen for him as a teenager and, again, in college. But she was a grown up now.

"Mr. Brewster, it's nice to finally meet you."

"Jeff, and the same here."

Lauren joined Jeff on the porch, where he loomed over her. While Jesse was wiry and compact, the only word for his father was *big*. Tall, muscular, a tad on the heavy side. *Big*.

"I'm sure Jesse will be right back from wherever he is."

"About that. He's not exactly expecting me today, and I haven't been able to get hold of him on the phone."

"Oh." Lauren unlocked the front door. "I was stopping by to let the dog out. Do you want to come in and get out of the heat? It's a scorcher today." She held the door open. "Go ahead." *Who besides the weather person said scorcher?* Lauren silently asked Jeff's back before following him in.

Xena rushed him, jumping up and licking his face.

"Down." Lauren ordered.

"It's okay," Jeff said. "Dogs and babies love me."

"I'm going to put her out back. That's what I stopped by for."

"Sure, I don't want to keep you. You're probably on your lunch break from work."

Lauren grabbed Xena's collar. "Have you had lunch? I was going to make myself something while I was here."

"I can go out for something." Jeff glanced around the room. "It's enough that you're letting Jesse and Shelley and me stay here."

"Lunch is no problem. And you and Jesse and the baby are staying next door in my mother's larger side of the house."

"Ah. I thought. Never mind."

Thought what? That Jesse was staying here with her? Lauren welcomed Xena's yank at her collar. "Yes, I'll let you out, girl." She looked up at Jeff. "You can make yourself comfortable here or come into the kitchen."

Jeff followed her and sat at the table while she let Xena out.

"Why don't you give Jesse another try?" Lauren asked as she opened the refrigerator to take out the sandwich fixings. "I know you're anxious to see him."

"And Shelley. I can't believe I have a granddaughter."

Lauren bit back her words of caution about assuming Shelley was Jesse's.

Jeff tried calling Jesse again. "It's going right to his voicemail now." He frowned.

Lauren placed lunch on the table and sat across from Jeff.

"You doing his legal stuff?" Jeff asked. "How's it going? How's my boy"

As tempting and exasperating as ever. Jesse's father had caught her off guard with his last question.

"I'm probating Shelley's mother's will and handling the prep for the guardianship hearing. Jesse had the DNA testing done a few days ago."

"Good."

"I also reviewed the business agreement between him and my mother." *But that was more for Mom's protection.*

Jeff didn't seem to notice she hadn't addressed his last question.

"He, Jesse, seemed better when we talked, psyched about his inheritance, for what it's worth, the deal with your mother. Starting over." Jeff raised his gazed expectantly.

He had noticed that she'd ignored his question. Lauren swallowed her mouthful of sweet tea.

"The accident. It almost did him in."

Lauren froze. She'd known it had ended his racing, but based on the information she'd been able to get from Mac, the racing team owner, it hadn't sounded life threatening.

"I hadn't realized it was that bad. He didn't contact me, wouldn't take my calls. Blocked my calls." She hated the tremor in her voice. Next thing she knew she'd be tearing up. She pressed her back straight against the chair. "It was like he'd dropped off the face of the earth." And she'd let him. By then, the distance, being apart so much had taken a toll on their relationship. A two-ton weight pushed against her sternum.

Jeff held her gaze with his. "In a way he had. But it was the end of his career, not the severity of the physical injury that knocked him for a loop. Shelley, my Shelley, needing him brought him back. For a while. You know, he spent nearly every penny he had saved up for the future helping me with his mother's medical expenses."

"That sounds like Jesse." Her mind drifted back to a much younger Jesse who'd tried to pay her room and board expenses at Syracuse University when her father had refused to.

"Yep." Pride sounded in Jeff's voice. "When we lost his mother, he really spiraled. I didn't hear from him for months. I don't know, don't care where he was, what he was doing, only that when he found out about his inheritance from his Uncle Jim, he came back to his old self."

The weight dropped to her stomach, setting off another flash of Jesse's kiss. But she'd moved on with her life, such that it was. She couldn't let what they'd once had exist as anything more than a memory.

"Jess seemed to think that since Jim was Shelley's uncle, the inheritance was some kind of kick in the pants from his mother to shape up and make something of his life." Jeff stared at his hands. "She was always better at that than I was."

"I don't know what to say." She'd heard enough from Jesse about how his dad was bound and determined for him to finish college, make something of himself better than a bike shop owner.

"Tell me to mind my own business, if you want. But why did you just let him go? Shelley and I thought you two had something special."

So had she. "You'll have to ask him," she ground out. "He's the one who called it quits."

Jeff's eyes lit. "Then, there still might be something between you?"

"Hello." Jesse's call through the front door saved her from answering that question for his father. Or for herself.

Jesse didn't wait for an answer to his shout out before letting himself and Shelley in. He'd seen his dad's rig on the street and Lauren's, but not Sonja's, car in the driveway. If Dad wasn't with Lauren, maybe she knew where he was. He hoisted Shelley on his hip. And maybe he could find out if she was actually avoiding him or it was his imagination. If she was avoiding him, that could be a good sign. It could mean she'd gotten the same jolt out of their kiss he had.

He wasn't going to assess how her avoidance could be a bad thing.

"In the kitchen," Lauren called.

She had the table set and sandwiches out for herself and his dad.

"Dad, hey, this a surprise. I wasn't expecting you yet."

"A good surprise, I hope." His dad's laughter had a questioning edge to it, something that wouldn't have been there before Mom …

"The best," Jesse said.

Lauren rose "Have you two had lunch? I can make more sandwiches."

"No, sit. We've eaten."

"`Donalds," Shelley said, showing Lauren her juice box.

She was so cute, Jesse just wanted to hug her, all the time. He rolled his shoulders. He was becoming his mother, an old woman, about Shelley. Not that his mother would have been old. But the cute. The hugging. That seemed to be something she would do. He wished his mom could have met her namesake.

"Who dat?" Shelley saved him from his emasculating analysis.

"That's your grandpa." The way his dad's eyes lit and face softened when he looked at Shelley took dead aim on his heart.

"Pa?" the little girl asked.

Jesse placed his hand on his father's shoulder. A shoulder just as broad and muscled as it had been when Jesse was Shelley's age. His gaze traced the age lines his mother's death had etched on Dad's face and took in the slight hunch in the way Dad carried himself. "My daddy," he said.

"Jesse-daddy daddy?" Shelley touched Jeff, too.

That was good, wasn't it? She didn't seem afraid of Dad. Just couldn't figure out who he was.

"Sit," Lauren said, pointing at the chair between her and Dad. "Can I at least get you sweet tea?"

He pulled out the chair and sat with his daughter on his lap. "Tea sounds good. Shelley understands grandma, but evidently not grandpa," he explained.

"Gammy home?" Shelley asked.

"Nope, she's still at work. Shelley calls Lauren's mother Grammy," he clarified for his father.

Dad raised an eyebrow toward Lauren, and she dropped her gaze to study her sandwich.

Jesse continued as if he hadn't see his father's gesture. "Shelley's m-o-t-h-e-r spent a lot of her childhood in foster care. Maybe she stayed in contact with one of her female foster parents. There's a lot I don't know." He took a sip of the tea Lauren had placed in front of him. "Like I don't know how you got here so fast. Dad, you did stop and sleep? Several times, I hope." When had he become the father here? Shelley squirmed on his lap, reminding him at least one way.

"Yes, I stopped, but not as many times as I would have if I hadn't had a second driver. I had no problem lining up someone for the condo. Then, one of my neighbors said his grandson was heading back here for summer classes. He goes to the University of South Carolina. Saved him the airfare by giving him a ride and having him share the driving with me."

Relief flowed through Jesse. "Good deal."

Lauren stood, the hint of her scent reminding him that she was still here, next to him. As if he could forget.

"I'd better get back to the office. You guys can leave the dishes in the sink and lock up on your way out, if you would."

"You might want to stay a few minutes." Lauren's mother appeared in the kitchen doorway waving a business-size envelope. "I ran into the mail deliverer on my way in."

"Gammy!" Shelley hopped off his lap grabbed Sonja's hand and pulled her over to the space between him and his dad. She reached up and touched his dad's beard. "Pa."

Sonja smiled at Jesse. "This must be your father."

"Jesse-daddy Daddy," Shelley confirmed.

"Hi, I'm Sonja Cooper." She offered her hand.

His father stood. "Jeff Brewster." He shook hands.

"I really do need to get back," Lauren said, pushing her chair to the table.

"You might want to call Brittany and tell her you're meeting with a client," Sonja said.

Jesse caught the City of Indigo Bay logo on the envelope Sonja waved again.

"This was forwarded from the Morrison property, I should say Brewster property, address. I signed for it." Sonja placed the letter on the table in front of him. "I can take Shelley—she's probably ready for her n-a-p—and show Jeff where he can unpack his stuff."

Was a letter from the city that big a deal? It looked innocuous enough to him. Or did Sonja know something he didn't. Either way, it would give him some time alone with Lauren. "You go ahead, Dad. I put my trailer in the back behind the garage. There's room for yours."

"Okay, don't let anyone say Jeff Brewster turned down an invitation from a beautiful woman."

Jesse started. He knew his dad was kidding and complementing his hostess. Mom was gone. It shouldn't matter if he wasn't. But it still did on some level, like it was some kind of betrayal. He knew all about betraying someone.

His father followed Sonja and Shelley, who'd gone readily to Sonja's arms.

Jesse slipped his forefinger under the flap of the envelop. "So, do you think this is as important as your mother made out, or her ploy to get my father alone?"

Lauren laughed. "More a ploy to leave us alone." She bit her lip as if she regretted her quip.

"She's succeeded." He held her gaze as long as he could before removing the letter from the envelope. He could leverage having Lauren all to himself after reading what the city wanted with him. Maybe, it was a welcome letter. Didn't small towns do stuff like that? Jesse studied the city logo. Probably not with a signed delivery receipt requested.

The quarter pounder in his stomach did a roundhouse kick as he skimmed down the page. *No.* They couldn't do this to him. Not when he had people depending on him—Shelley, Dad, Sonja. People he couldn't let down. He'd done enough of that in the past. Jesse tore his gaze from the letter and looked across the table at Lauren.

"What? That bad?" she asked.

"That bad. The city is condemning my property."

"Let me see that." Lauren reached over and took the sheet, her fingers brushing his. She discounted the tingle that ran up her arm as apprehension about Jesse's situation and read the letter. "Not if you can get your plans for the renovation to the city planning board by the next planning board meeting." She swallowed. "Next week."

Jesse's grim expression didn't change. "Yeah, plans signed off on by an engineer. You know that train pulled out long ago. Pun intended."

Eyes lowered, Lauren tapped the tabletop with her fingernail. How willing was she to go all out to help Jesse? She'd kept telling herself it would be best for everyone, for her, if he sold out and left Indigo Bay. But, even with the beachfront, he'd get far less for a condemned property than he would for the property renovated, or even for the real estate alone. And she doubted Jesse had the means to take down the house. Plus there was her mother and her investment in the property—emotional and financial.

"That might not be a problem. I know someone who would review your plans, give you any needed revisions, and sign off."

"An old boyfriend?" Jesse's grin didn't make his eyes.

Lauren's heart skipped a beat. "Engineers don't have to be men." She covered for her traitorous emotions. Jesse's question couldn't mean anything. He was just frustrated.

"You did see the time frame for compliant completion?" he asked.

Lauren reread the letter. "It's tight. What if you hired more help?"

Jesse fisted and released his fingers. "There's a little matter of money to consider. The agreement with your mother has a limited amount of money for labor, other than my free services."

"The high school kids are out for the summer. I can check at church to see if any are still looking for summer work. And to be as sexist as you were about engineers, you could ask your dad for his help and hire a teen girl to take care of Shelley for a lot less than you'd have to pay a construction worker."

He shoved his hands into the front pockets of his jeans. "I'd have to talk things over with your mother. See if the project is still doable from her financial perspective." He scrubbed his palms over his face. "Maybe I should just consider that offer from your boss or whoever."

"If the offer still stands since the city moved toward condemnation."

His shoulders sagged.

Lauren could have slapped herself. Jesse didn't need any more dumped on him.

He pushed away from the table. "I'd better let you get back to work and see if Dad needs any help settling in."

"I am working. You're one of our clients." But she wasn't going to try to kid herself that the only reason she was helping Jesse was because he was a client. Nor was she going to try to figure why right now. "I'll go back to the office and call Cara about looking at your plans."

Jesse's mouth curled into a smile. "So your engineering friend is a woman."

"Both, actually. It's a husband-wife professional corporation. I met them at a trivia night at the sports grill when I first moved here. They were new to town, too, and we were put together in a pick-up team." Lauren snapped her mouth shut. Why was she rambling on? The only answer that came to mind was that she didn't want to leave. "I'll also check into why you, the estate, didn't receive more notice on the condemnation, and get back to you."

Rather than leave, Jesse waited while she rose and collected her things. He walked with her to the door.

"You do that." His low voice, warm breath in her ear was as potent as a kiss.

Lauren grabbed for the door handle to steady herself and grabbed dead air.

Jesse took her by the elbow. "You okay? If you don't want to handle this, my legal stuff, I can call and ask for one of your bosses to represent me."

"Don't do that." Had Jesse picked up the self-doubt in her strident response?

"Not like you aren't doing a good job."

Lauren fought the insecurity tearing through her, about her job, her relationship—whatever it might be—with Jesse.

"I was thinking more like our relationship is too close," Jesse said.

His eyes darkened, forcing her to lean more heavily on him, since her legs weren't doing any job of supporting her.

"That could be worse," Lauren said before she realized she'd vocalized her thought. "Professionalism and all that." And the secretive way the Morrison estate had been settled. Lauren hated to think it, but she didn't know if her bosses could fairly represent Jesse's interests, given their close ties to Ken Kostner. It wouldn't be intentional. Bile burned the back of her throat. Or, at least she didn't think it would be.

"Not to mention the potential for gossip getting out," she blurted to fill the sound void caused by her retreat into her thoughts about work. "You remember how it was with us back in Chenango Falls?"

He squeezed her arm, sending a shiver through her, despite the blast of afternoon heat coming through the now-open door.

"I remember."

The shiver went into overdrive. Yeah, she remembered, too.

CHAPTER 8

Jesse had heard from Lauren's engineer friends by yesterday afternoon and emailed them his plans, but he hadn't heard back from her, which gave him a bad feeling. And it hadn't raised his spirits this morning when he'd gone to the local home improvement store with Sonja's notarized document to open a line of credit for the materials they'd need to get started on the work and had been told Sonja would have to come in herself to set up the line.

"Jesse-Daddy home," Shelley said with a flying leap into his arms when he walked into Sonja's duplex. It squeezed his heart at how quickly the little girl had attached herself to him and Sonja and living here. He hoped the adjustment to moving to the cottage, their own place, would be as smooth. He hugged her to him. That was a concern for the future. He had enough immediate ones. He hadn't gotten his DNA results yet, either.

"Are we ready to get going?" His dad rose from the recliner where he'd been reading to Shelley. "Sonja's finished her showing and is on her way home to stay with Shelley."

"About that." Jesse explained about the line of credit and materials. "I hope we don't lose all of today." He didn't add that he hadn't a minute, let alone whole day to spare, if they were going to meet the time frame of the condemnation notice and establish their residence in the cottage for the approval of his guardianship of Shelley.

"Maybe this is better news." His father reached down and picked up an envelope from the table next to the chair.

Jesse's windpipe constricted so he couldn't draw a full breath when he caught the return address on the mail. The testing facility in Charleston. Had Lauren gotten her copy at the office yesterday? Was that why she hadn't contacted him? She didn't want to be the bearer of bad news. He squeezed Shelley to him again.

"Too tight." She pushed at him. "Down."

He placed her on the floor. *No.* Fierce denial ran through him. He knew she was his, like he'd once known Lauren was his.

His phone pinged in his pocket. Who would be texting him, except Lauren? Jesse forced air into his lungs as he pulled the phone from his pocket.

Good news. Call me.

"Lauren. She wants to talk." He slapped the unopened envelop against his thigh.

"Go ahead," his dad said. "Shelley and I will finish our story."

"Pa, story." She pointed at the book.

He bent and kissed her soft curls. "I'll be right back after I make my phone call." Jesse stepped into the hall to the kitchen.

"Hey!" Lauren answered. "I've got some information for you."

"About the DNA testing? I got something from the center today, but I haven't opened it."

"That and the condemnation notice."

It might be the connection, but to him it sounded liked she lowered her voice for the second half of her reply.

"I know you and your dad planned to work today, but can we get together first?"

"Sure." He leaned his shoulder against the wall. His dad could watch Shelley and Sonja could go set up the line of credit at the home improvement store. "What time do you want me there?"

"Not here. I could use some time out of the office. I'll come to you at the house. And go ahead and open the letter from the testing center."

"All right!" Lauren wouldn't be encouraging him to open the letter if it wasn't something good.

"See you in about a half hour," she said.

Lauren hung up, and Jesse tore open the envelope. He read down the sheet. "She *is* mine. I knew it," he whispered.

"Did you say something?" his dad asked.

He looked up from the letter. "The DNA test. Shelley's mine." If it weren't a chick thing, he'd say he was giddy.

"I knew that," his dad said. "Didn't you?"

"Yeah." He *had* known in his heart. "But I have it in writing now."

"So, this wraps it up? The guardianship. You're her father. You don't need to be named her guardian."

"I'm not sure it's that easy. Lauren will tell me when she gets here."

"Lauren's coming here? You're not going to her office?"

Spoken aloud, it sounded a little strange for just a business relationship.

"Tell you what. When Sonja gets here, we'll take Shelly and go to the home improvement center and get that line of credit straightened out."

Leaving him and Lauren alone in the house. "Works for me."

Sonja rushed in the front door. "Sorry, I'm later than I said. Caroline called. She may have someone to watch Shelley for you. I've got the information on my phone." She fumbled in her purse for it.

His dad stood, Shelley on his hip, and touched Sonja's arm. "You can give him the sitter information when we get back."

Sonja gave his father a warm smile so like one Jesse had seen on Lauren's face for him many times in the past.

"Back from where?" Sonja asked.

"The home improvement center. I'll fill you in in the car. Lauren will be here in a few minutes to talk with Jesse. He got the results from the DNA test."

"From your faces, I'd say good news."

"The best," Jesse said, his voice hitching.

"So, lets you and me and my granddaughter head to the store and give Jesse and Lauren some *privacy* to talk legal stuff."

His father exchanged what could only be called a private smile with Sonja. They were smiling about him and Lauren? He studied the pair. *Not entirely*, from the low charge electricity in the air. Sonja and Dad? He'd think about that later, maybe throw out the possibility to Lauren that something might be developing between their parents. More likely he was thinking in that direction because that's where his thoughts kept going about him and Lauren.

Jesse leaned over and gave Shelley a peck on the cheek. "You be a good girl for Grandpa at the store, and I'll see you when you get back."

"Good girl, Pa." The little girl nodded emphatically.

Jesse watched the trio leave, reread the DNA results unable to resist a fist pump, and then paced the living room a couple times before heading to the kitchen to put on a fresh pot of coffee. That done, he checked the kitchen clock and took the cinnamon rolls he'd picked up at Caroline's out of the bag on the counter, warmed them in the microwave, and arranged and rearranged them on a plate on the kitchen table. He frowned. He was turning into a regular cooking show competitor. *Presentation is everything.*

Jesse added plates for them to the table, along with sugar and creamer. There was nothing wrong with a little party to celebrate good news. Besides, it wasn't that he didn't have party experience of all kinds— participant and organizer. Memories of the Team Macachek Christmas party Lauren's aunt had pushed them together to organize flooded his head. It had been an obvious ploy to get them together after an earlier breakup. A ploy that had worked at the time.

That team party had been the last one Lauren had gone to. He blinked, but the pictures wouldn't go away. She'd been drop dead gorgeous, her glittery teal dress falling softly from her bare shoulders to just above her knees, clinging in all the right places to emphasize her curves. They'd danced to what had been *their* song. "I'll Wait for You." He'd promised he would. And he hadn't. A lump formed in his throat. In truth, it had been more of a disappearing act on his part after the accident. But it looked the same. When she'd finished college and law school, he hadn't been there.

But that race had already finished, and he couldn't change the results. The DNA test results were something else, something to celebrate, as was the possible sitter for Shelley, and his dad being here for him. Despite the crunch placed on him by the condemnation notice, for the first time since his racing accident, Jesse felt he had a future ahead of him, both personal and professional. He heard a car pull into the driveway.

And he wasn't going to let anything stop him from going full throttle into that future.

Lauren nibbled her bottom lip as she pulled open the screen door to her mother's side of the duplex. She knew all the legalities of condemnation proceedings. Acer and Acer sometimes consulted on behalf of the city on them. She knew estate law. The firm had taken all the right steps. But the Morrison file didn't have any notices in it.

She stepped into the empty living room. When Lauren had called the planning board secretary, the woman had said the discussion of the condemnation was in one of the board's earlier meeting minutes. The secretary was sure the city attorney's office had drafted the intent notice shortly afterwards to be sent to Mr. Morrison's executor or heir, depending on whether or not the estate had been settled when the notice had been sent, and to the local newspaper.

Lauren's follow-up with the city clerk had confirmed that the condemnation hearing notice had been posted in the paper and that the other notice should have been mailed the same day. The clerk had offered to get Lauren dates, but Lauren had said she could just as easily check the newspaper. The woman had gone on about how sad it was that neither Mr. Morrison's heir or representative had come to the initial condemnation hearing and that "the lovely old mansion" had been allowed to deteriorate. The clerk had wished Lauren luck when she'd said Jesse wanted to save it.

"Anyone here?" Lauren called. Jesse's and his dad's trucks were both parked out front.

"I'll be down in a minute." Jesse's voice came down the stairs.

That would give her a little more time to couch how to ask Jesse and, maybe better, his dad if any notices had been sent to their California home. It was possible the notice had been sent to Jesse at his California residence, and not Acer and Acer, if the estate had already been settled. Both of the Acer brothers had curtly told her all the documents pertaining to the Morrison estate they'd received were in the work folder. She'd attributed the curtness of their replies to Jesse not jumping at Ken Kostner's offer or her not pushing the sale hard enough to him. From the dates of the newspaper posting, the estate could have already been settled when the city sent the notice, which meant it would have gone to Jesse.

Jesse had said the estate was settled six months ago. But the deed to the property hadn't been updated until she'd done it after Jesse had arrived in Indigo Bay. No matter how she framed the question to Jesse in her head on the drive over, in the context of the information she'd gotten, it sounded like either her accusing him of blowing off the notice or some kind of conspiracy on the part of the city and Acer and Acer. But that was ridiculous. Acer and Acer was a well-respected firm. Or it had been. Her thoughts went to the firm's lack of recent new business.

"Hey, you here with me?"

Jesse's tease brought her out of her internal fog. *A conspiracy, right.* She'd been reading too many suspense novels. "I was thinking."

"About me?"

"Yes."

"Good thoughts? I couldn't tell from your expression."

"About your legal situation, the condemnation,"

"Of course."

Jesse shot her a lopsided grin that could have been a further tease or a cover for the uncertainty she'd glimpsed in his eyes. If that's what she'd glimpsed.

Whatever, the smile knocked her heart off-kilter and drawn her to the symmetry of his lips. Lips that had felt like coming home when he'd pressed them to hers the other evening. Maybe Jesse had been right when he'd said he could ask one of the partners to take over for her. Maybe they were too close, or still too attracted to each other, too affected by their past.

"I think you've gone missing again." He took her elbow. "What did you have for breakfast? I'd like to think my very presence sends you into a dreamlike state, but on past experience, more likely you're hungry."

"A cup of coffee. I was rushed this morning."

"Have just the thing for you, then."

That's what she was afraid of.

He guided her to the kitchen. "Fresh coffee and cinnamon rolls from Caroline's. Nothing like some caffeine and sugar to get your metabolism buzzing."

Between the memories she could no longer keep compartmentalized in her mind and his warm fingers on her arm, she was already buzzing more than she needed or wanted to be. She had to get back on track with the business-like meeting she'd planed on the drive over. The cozy table for two with settings placed next to each other, rather than across the table didn't help.

"Go ahead and sit," Jesse said. "I'll get us each a mug of coffee."

The sweet cinnamon aroma of the rolls made her stomach gurgle in hunger. "Excuse me." Or was it nerves about asking Jesse about the earlier condemnation notice? When had she ever been afraid to ask Jesse anything? Then again, when had his answer to a question put so much at stake for so many people—his and his daughter's livelihood, her mother's finances, her job.

That is, if Jesse hadn't read or had blown off a prior notice.

She swallowed the bitter taste in her mouth. The Acers were crafty in serving their more favored clients, like Ken, but not dishonest. With Ken interested in buying the mansion property and not knowing what Jesse's plans were if he did, she could see the brothers shrugging off the condemnation notice in the newspaper. She'd been trained better than to assume wrongdoing on circumstantial evidence.

"Here you go." He placed her mug in from of her and slid into the chair next to her, yanking his thigh away when it brushed hers. "I, uh, thought sitting next to each other would be better if you have documents or whatever for me to look at with you."

Jesse was concerned about the place settings looking like he was making a move on her? Lauren hadn't seen the degree of uncertainty she'd caught in his eyes earlier in years, probably not since their first kiss at seventeen.

"And here I thought it was to get close to me."

His eyes widened, and one corner of his mouth tipped up.

She had said her thought aloud and, worse, had warmed to his efforts.

Lauren cleared her throat and stirred creamer into her coffee before taking a sip. "I need to ask you an important question."

Jesse raised an eyebrow.

"One I need you to answer, even if the answer doesn't show you in a good light."

"If it's about why I left you. Truthfully, I wasn't myself after my accident and Mom's death. I am now. If I could have a do over, I'd handle things differently. I still l …"

Lauren called on all of the strength she had to lift her hand and press her fingers to his lips to stop Jesse from finishing. Her emotions about him, her unfounded suspicions, her career were too jumbled to hear what she knew he was going to say.

"Before the estate was settled, did you receive any notices about the possible condemnation of your uncle's property before the one you received here." *There.* She'd gotten the question out in a professional tone despite Jesse's almost declaration and his warm breath on her fingertips having reduced her insides to mush.

"Not what I was expecting," he said with a sheepish grin.

Lauren gripped her mug like the coffee was her lifeblood. "Did you? Could you have tossed it unread?"

Jesse leaned back in his seat and crossed his arms. "I did not. Why?"

"The planning board secretary said the city attorney drafted a notice about the original condemnation meeting to be mailed to you or to Acer and Acer, if the estate was still in settlement when it was sent. We don't have that notice in your file at work."

He unfolded his arms. "When I was at my worst, I didn't care enough about my mail to go through it to throw something out. Anyway, wouldn't the notice come signed receipt required? The one here did. Your mother signed the delivery confirmation."

"Maybe that was because it was a second notice, because you didn't show up at the original meeting?"

Jesse pushed away from the table and walked to the coffee maker to refill his mug. "Because I didn't know about it. Or try this: Because it didn't require a signature, the first notice got lost in the mail and no one knew that."

She picked up a crumb from her cinnamon roll off the table and dropped it on her plate, unable to meet his eyes. "I didn't consider that."

He leaned against the counter. "Look at me. Please.

She lifted her head.

"Since I found out about my inheritance, I've wanted it more than anything I've wanted in a good long time, except the people I care for. I've blown enough important things in my life and regretted it." Jesse paused.

Lauren's heart slammed against her chest at the thought that she might be one of those important things.

"I wouldn't have blown this. If you're looking for someone to blame, look closer."

Her lungs constricted. Bottom line, the only one closer was her mother. "Mom is on *your* side of this."

"We have sides? Which side are you on? By closer, I meant your law practice."

"I … I thought … they wouldn't." She straightened in the chair. *There was no conspiracy, only some kind of mix up, or several mix-ups.* "I'm not looking to place blame, and it's not my law firm. I'm not a partner."

"But you want to be."

"That's my plan." *Or it was.* Since Jesse had arrived in Indigo Bay, her whole life had been upended. And she didn't like it. It stretched the boundaries of her neat little comfort zone.

"At any cost?"

"Of course not." She rolled her shoulders to counter the itch between her shoulder blades. "Do you want someone else to represent you?

"I want a lot of things. Working with either of your partners isn't one of them."

"There are other law firms in town."

"What are we doing here?" Jesse scraped his hand through his hair. "Isn't it time we laid this disagreement to rest. Your career versus my career, or lack of one."

She dropped her chin to her chest. The uneasiness at work lately, the thoughts she'd had about her bosses. What career? Maybe she was the one with no career future.

Jesse stepped over and squeezed her shoulder. The soft look on his face lifted some of the weight from her chest.

"I'm not chasing fame anymore. Not with Shelley, Dad, the agreement with your mother about the property."

Despite looking a little forced, his grin shot straight to her heart.

"You, me. We're both chasing security. Wouldn't we be more of a force working together?"

The truth of his statement, her longing for an earlier time, to be one with Jesse, obliterated everything else in her mind. Lauren stood, wrapped her arms around

Jesse's waist, and placed her head against his chest. His heartbeat was rivaling hers for a new speed record. "Yes, a formidable force."

He lifted her chin. Let's do it then. And when all this legal stuff is done …"

He brushed her lips with a whisper of a kiss that left her longing for me. So much more.

"We have something else to settle."

Lauren didn't know whether to take that as a threat or a promise, so she lost herself in the strength of his arms so she didn't have to think about it.

CHAPTER 9

"Do you have a minute?" Ray caught Lauren on her way to relieve Brittany on the front desk so the legal assistant could take her lunch break.

"Brittany's going on her lunch break." She bit her tongue. Ray would certainly think anything he had to say to her was more important than her coworker's lunch. And in the great scheme of things, it probably was.

"Brittany," he shouted up the hall. "Lauren will be there in a couple minutes. Ray motioned her into his office. "No need to sit. As I told Brittany, this will only take a minute."

Lauren pasted what she hoped was in interested-looking smile on her face. She hadn't abandoned all hope of becoming partner or wanting to become partner, despite her uneasy feelings about her bosses.

"I saw that the DNA results come in on the Brewster case."

She shifted her weight from foot to foot. "Yes, indicating Mr. Brewster is the father."

"Good. That should simplify the guardianship review." He rubbed his hands together.

She couldn't block the picture in her mind of some weaselly cartoon character doing the same with an evil grin on his face. Ray's expression was neutral.

"You've got the hearing on the docket?"

"Yes, moved up to tomorrow morning. A scheduled case settled out of court. Judge Trexler's assistant called me earlier today to see if we could be ready." She'd automatically said "yes," but hadn't heard back from Jesse yet.

"Even better. Get that and the planning commission hearing wrapped up."

Wrapping up the legal part of her relationship with Jesse wasn't a problem. It was the personal, family loose ends that were whipping in the wind.

"We need your time free to work with Ken on a new development project he's launching."

"Ken Kostner?"

"Who else?"

Every muscle in her body locked in joint step. "Here in Indigo Bay?" One by one, her muscles relaxed after her question came out in a normal, casual tone, rather than the way the words had screamed through her head first.

"It's a new joint venture with another firm in Charleston."

That didn't exactly answer her question. Maybe, she should ask why Ray was anxious to close the Jesse's case. *No.* That would get her the same distain that her "Ken who" question had.

"And before I forget. You asked about the Morrison estate receiving notice of the property condemnation meeting. The notice was after the estate had been settled. The city clerk reminded me that the notice was published in the newspaper at the same time, and I checked the dates. We didn't receive any notice. But your client should have. If he didn't know, it was no fault of ours or the clerk's office."

Ray had investigated her question? To what end? Cover the firm? From what? And whose fault had it been? She was veering dangerously close to the edge of conspiracy again. The reason why flashed in her mind. She didn't want it to be Jesse's fault. She wanted him to be the responsible person he said he was, was trying to be, now. Her mother's financial partner. A future business owner with his father if they opened the bike shop Jesse talked about.

"Brewster will have his say at the planning meeting. Either he can meet the time frame the board wants or he can't, and we can move on to other things."

But she wasn't ready for some of the things she had to move on to. "We should be able to negotiate a reasonable completion date. And he and his father are talking about opening another business in Indigo Bay. More business for the firm," she added to give some purpose to her words other than rooting for Jesse's success. Which she was.

"Good." Ray's voice was flat.

Ray's lack of any enthusiasm for the prospect of new business, considering the lack there of, except for Ken's new venture, ticked off Lauren. If she was going to make partner wanted to make partner, she had to expand her client base. But at the moment, she was about as enthused about that as Ray seemed to be.

"Keep me updated on the guardianship, when you can get to work with Ken."

"Will do, and the situation with the Morrison … Brewster property."

"Yeah, that too."

Ray shuffled the papers on his desk into a pile.

"I'll go relieve Brittany."

"Let her know that Gerry and I'll be out for the afternoon."

She wasn't aware that Gerry was in to be out. "Sure." She forced herself to take regular measured steps, rather than bolting from the weirdness that had descended on the firm—or, at least on her place in it.

"Here I am," she said as she stepped into the reception area.

"Great. I thought Ray was going to make me late for my nail appointment. They were able to squeeze me in on late notice."

Lauren took in the faint flush on her coworker's face. "Hot date tonight?"

"No. Sort of. My brother's former college roommate is in town, and my brother invited me to make a foursome with his girlfriend for dinner." Brittany grabbed her bag and grinned. "I've wanted to get to know this guy better forever, but he was engaged. And now he's not."

"Shoo," Lauren said. "Or you're going to make yourself late."

While Brittany left, Lauren went and got her lunch from the refrigerator in the employee room off reception. She opened the plastic salad container and Spider Solitaire on Brittany's computer for a mindless diversion from the thoughts ping ponging in her head. Thoughts that all had their roots in Jesse and her feelings for him. The feelings that no matter how much she tried to deny them, were as strong as they had ever been. Since she was alone in the office, she turned on the game's sound as if that could drown everything out.

"Hey."

Lauren jerked at Jesse's voice. She hadn't heard the door open or close. Guess the sound did drown out something. She licked her tongue across her teeth to make sure she didn't have a piece of spinach or something stuck in them, and her hands automatically smoothed her hair.

"Hey, yourself. What brings you here?"

"You called."

"You could have called back."

"But I couldn't have seen you then."

"You could have video called."

Jesse gave her a slow perusal that sent a tingle up her spine. "I couldn't have seen you *in person*."

Laure fidgeted in her chair. She had to put a stop to this conversation before it incinerated her. "I thought you and your dad were busy working today."

"I'm ever too busy for you."

Nor am I too busy for you, no matter how I try to be. "What I called about was that there's an unexpected opening on the court docket tomorrow, and the judge will hear our guardianship petition."

"Yes!" Jesse shouted, striding over and pulling her to her feet.

He gave her a quick smack on the lips that shouldn't have set fireworks off in her. But did. His joy was for Shelley, not for her. As it should be.

"Since you're here, I had a couple things I wanted to go over with you for court."

He let go of her. "Sure."

"First, we're scheduled for ten."

Jesse's phone rang. "I'd better see who this is. It could be Emma, Shelley's new babysitter, or something."

"Of course." *His daughter was his first priority.* But Lauren couldn't help remembering a time when she had held that place, ahead, sometimes even of his racing. A wash of what could only be called guilt flowed over her. She'd professed to love him, yet let her self-promise to never allow a man control her life as her father had controlled her mother's push Jesse to second on her priority list, after her college and career ambitions.

Pfft. Lauren glanced sidewise to see if Jesse had heard her. He was busy listening to his phone call. Career didn't seem so all important now. As Jesse had said, promised, after their legal business was settled …

He ended the call. "I've got to go. Dad's run into a problem."

"And he needs you." She took measure of him, his broad shoulder, muscled forearms, the strength she knew he wielded inside and out.

Didn't they all?

～

"All done. Cookie." Shelley held up her empty dinner plate to Jesse.

He couldn't contain his goofy grin as Judge Trexler's words from yesterday morning replayed in his head, "under parental rights, Jesse Brewster's guardianship and provisional custody of the minor child, Shelley Cavanaugh is confirmed."

One down. Although he had to "establish" them in their own household as part of the provisions that would get him permanently out from under the supervision of Child Protective Services. Something about Sonja's duplex having insufficient bedrooms for three adults and a child. But he had a month to do that, and the engineer's inspection had found that, unlike the main house, the cottage didn't have any structural damage. It only needed a deep cleaning, cosmetic repairs, and child proofing to make an acceptable home.

One to go. The planning board meeting tonight. He took the plate from Shelley, and she hopped down from the chair.

"Free." She held up all of her fingers.

"Two. One for each hand," he countered.

She grabbed them. "Okay. Cure-us George."

"The Curious George DVD I picked up today," Sonja said. "Emma brought one of her little sister's the other day, and Shelley couldn't stop talking about it."

Emma. The babysitter. Guilt tugged at him. He hadn't seen her since he'd hired her. He and Dad had been leaving for the worksite early, before Sonja and working as long as they had natural light. He would have worked longer, except the electricity wasn't on in either structure and he wanted to limit use of the generator to their power tools to save money. Jesse was only home for supper today because of the planning board meeting. He glanced at Shelley gazing up at him expectantly.

"Daddy-Jesse. Cure-us George?"

Before he could answer, his father scooped her up and tickled her belly with his nose.

"Remember, your daddy has his meeting tonight."

Dad had talked to Shelley about his meeting? He had a lot to learn about this parenting stuff.

"Grandma and I'll watch your movie with you," Jesse's dad said.

"'Kay, Pa."

"Jesse, go ahead and get ready. We have this covered."

He did as his dad had said. He did need to clean up more and change out of his work clothes. There'd be more time later, after the renovations were done and their future was secured. He'd be there for Shelley more then, make it up to her. His pulse throbbed in his throat. Like he'd promised himself about Lauren when he'd been at the top of his racing career? Jesse rolled his shoulders. But he and Lauren had another chance now—a chance he'd also put off for the renovations.

Jesse fastened the top button of his shirt, ran his finger around the inside of the collar, and looked at the tie on the bed. He hated anything tight around his neck. Anything except Lauren's arms. But this evening was business, not about them. He needed to look like the businessman he wanted to be.

"Jesse," Sonja called up the stairs. "Lauren is here."

He tied the tie and grabbed his sports jacket from the closet, folding it over his arm. It had to still be 90 degrees outside. Maybe he didn't need to wear a jacket.

He'd ask Lauren. He bounded down the stairs to see Lauren all suited up. But her black suit had short sleeves. His gaze dropped. And it looked like she had one of those light almost nothing sleeveless shirts underneath. He swallowed. Her straight skirt molded her curves, ending at her knees. *Business. Keep your mind on business.*

"Hey," Jesse said as he pulled on the jacket. Lauren had him on the edge of an inferno. What would another few degrees matter?

"Ready?" she asked.

"Yep." But not necessarily for what she was asking. He picked up the leather case with a copy of the project plans that Sonja had lent him. The engineer would have a copy, too, but he figured if he was masquerading as a businessman, he might as well go all out.

"Looking good," she said when they stepped out onto the front porch.

Jesse preened. So, he wasn't the only one doing some checking out.

"I don't think I've seen you this dressed up since …" Lauren stopped mid-step and cleared her throat. "Since the last team Christmas party we went to." She strode ahead to her car.

Was she thinking of the promise he'd given her that night, too? He opened the passenger side door and slid in, shifting in the seat as she drove toward the city hall in silence. "Mind if I put the radio on?" he asked a few blocks into the drive.

"Go ahead." The silence broken, she continued. "Have you changed your mind and contacted the police about what happened at the mansion the other day as I'd advised you to?"

"No."

Her question irritated him, which it shouldn't. She was only acting as his attorney, keeping their relationship professional. But he didn't want to pack on more legal entanglements. He wanted their professional relationship to be wrapped up, end tonight with the planning board meeting, so they could pursue their personal relationship.

"As I told you, it was nothing—a can of gas. Probably, some kid's four-wheeler or bike ran out nearby. It was an easy refill, what with Dad leaving the can out next to the portable generator where it could be seen from the gate while he grabbed lunch on the boardwalk. I'm not proud of it, but I'll admit it's something I might have done as a teen."

What he wasn't going to admit was that the gas can had reappeared today while he and Dad were at lunch. Full. Dad had thought it was the person returning the gas, but something had made Jesse check it before they used it. The gas had been cut with water and something gritty—a mixture that could have killed the generator and cost them both money and time.

"All right. I won't press it." Lauren took a turn sharp right. "To change topics, tonight should be straight forward. Cara will present her engineering report and your plans, and we'll negotiate a rehabilitation agreement with the board."

"Yeah, I understand that." He didn't know why Lauren was telling him what they'd already discussed, except it was a neutral topic. Jesse studied her profile out of the corner of his eye. Her facial muscles were relaxed. His chest tightened. Maybe she was reassuring him. "And I want to hold fast to the six to eight months' time frame for completion."

"Right, I can't see that being a problem." Lauren pulled into parking place in front of the city hall.

He looked around at the other empty parking spaces. "Doesn't look like a large crowd."

"Shouldn't be. We're the only ones on the agenda, and I can't see anyone opposing what you and Mom are doing. The Morrison mansion is a historical landmark around here. In fact, the city clerk told me she was pleased to hear you were going to fix it up, rather than tear it down and build."

"Sounds like someone good to have on our side." He opened the car door. "Let's go in and get this over with, so I can get down to work rebuilding."

A home and what we once had.

"Hi, Lauren." She and Jesse ran into Dallas Harper and one of the other planning board members, a crony of her bosses and Ken Kostner, in the city hall lobby on their way to the meeting room.

"Hi, Dallas. I want to thank you for the help and advice you've given Mom about the positives and pitfalls of running rental properties in Indigo Bay. It's really helped with her B&B project planning."

"No problem. It's not like her short-term rentals will cut into my cottage occupation." He laughed. "Besides, there are plenty of tourists for both of us, and then some."

Jesse nudged her with his elbow. "Where are my manners? Dallas Harper, this is Jesse Brewster, an old friend. Dallas owns and rents out those cute cottages along Seaside Boulevard. And this is…"

"Bill Crowley." The other man's hand shot out ahead of Dallas's to shake Jesse's hand.

Were all of Ray and Gerry's friends and clients obnoxious, or was she becoming more sensitive to it as her dissatisfaction with her job increased?

"I'm going to head in so we can get started," Dallas said.

"We all should," Lauren said.

Bill stood where he was, half blocking her and Jesse's way to the meeting room. "I'm surprised you're representing Brewster."

Lauren didn't have to be touching Jesse to feel his rigid stance.

"I don't know what you've heard about me, but Lauren …"

"Nothing about you, although you did have quite a reputation for a while in the racing circuits. No, I was talking about Lauren's conflict of interest."

Her conflict of interest?

"Acer and Acer is one of Indigo Bay's consulting legal advisors."

Jesse glanced at her, and a shadow passed over his face.

He couldn't think she'd do anything other than represent him with everything she had, could he?

His shoulders sagged.

Or, maybe he could, given the distance she'd created between them.

"If you mean the pro bono I do for the public defender's office in traffic court and minor criminal cases, there's no conflict."

"I didn't mean your pro bono work," Bill checked his watch. "We'd better get in for the meeting." He turned on his heel and strode away.

"What was that about?" Jesse asked.

"I seriously don't know."

Jesse's eyes narrowed a fraction, a small change that anyone who didn't know him well would miss.

"But I'm going to find out." Her words were a much for her as for Jesse. She'd hoped speaking her intentions would heal the cut of his doubts. But her wounds were still raw.

Lauren breathed a sigh of relief at the smiles and nods Jesse received from the board members when he followed the engineer's presentation with his project overview and financial details. From the way he straightened and the bounce in his step as he returned to the seat next to her, she was sure he'd read the board's reaction the same way.

"Thank you, Mr. Brewster," the board chair said. "We have no problem with your six-to-eight months completion date."

Jesse fairly vibrated next to her.

"However."

The vibrations stopped.

"The city's engineering firm has an interim requirement."

Lauren tensed, earning her a questioning look from Jesse. "Later," she whispered. The city's engineering firm was the same one Ken Kostner used for projects in this part of the state, and if she remembered correctly, the firm's owner was friendly with Bill. Talk about conflict of interest.

"The board wants to see the structural repairs needed on the main house done within six weeks."

Lauren watched Jesse's Adams apple bob as he swallowed. "I see." He ran his palms down his thighs under the table.

"Tell them about Shelley, the cottage," she urged.

"That's personal. I won't use her as a pawn to get what I want."

She couldn't see how explaining his situation would be using his daughter as a pawn. But she knew when Jesse dug his feet in, there was no moving him. That determination might be enough to meet the board's time frame.

"Do you have something more to add?" the chair asked.

"A question," Jesse said. "What's the rationale for the additional stipulation?"

"We're headed into peak tourist season. We want to be proactive against any accident the failing structure could cause if someone were to be on the property."

"Trespassing," Lauren said.

"Unfortunately, yes. And the city could have some liability because of the rehabilitation agreement. The engineering firm recommended only four weeks, but the board thought that was unreasonable."

Jesse nodded, his expression blank.

"What if Jesse keeps the front gate locked at all times?" Lauren shook off Jesse's frown. She was acting in his best interests.

"It's okay. We can do it with additional hired help." He squeezed her hand under the table, sending a red-hot flash up her arm that she was sure showed on her face." A glance at the board, showed all of them, except Bill, focused on Jesse.

"I'll sign the agreement," he said.

"The board secretary has a copy for you."

The woman Lauren had talked with on the phone when she was researching the condemnation notice walked over with a folder.

"Read it, and have your counsel read it." The chair nodded at Lauren. "You can return a notarized copy to the city clerk. Let me know if you want any substantive changes. The board will have to review them before it signs the agreement."

Lauren nodded as she shot her hand out to take the agreement, afraid Jesse would just sign it to get it over with. "If everything is agreeable, we should have your signed copy back first thing tomorrow morning."

Their business done, Lauren and Jesse left the city hall.

"Thanks," he said, holding the door open for her.

"For what?"

"Taking charge. I might have just signed the agreement to get it done and over with."

Lauren stepped outside warmed by the summer night air and Jesse's appreciation. "That's what you're paying me for."

Jesse let the door slam shut behind him.

Lauren's mood grayed. She'd mean her words as a tease.

"Back to your office to read the agreement?" he asked, all business, as she pressed the key fob to unlock her car.

"No, let's go to Caroline's. My treat." She smiled at him as she settled behind the steering wheel.

A quizzical look accompanied his return smile. "Sure." Had he picked up on her reluctance to conduct their legal business at the office? The odds were neither of the guys would be there, but she didn't know for sure. Sometimes, she felt Jesse knew her better than she did herself. Lauren pressed the gas harder than necessary to pull out of the parking space, earning her another questioning glance from Jesse.

"Did I tell you about my new project at work, once we review the agreement and my business with you is finished?" she asked to reroute any thoughts Jesse might have about going to Caroline's instead of her office before he asked questions.

"Nope, and our legal business isn't quite done. Shelley's last name still needs to be changed to Brewster."

"That's just a matter of filing, which I've already done. There's no reason your petition won't go through quickly."

"Sounds like you're anxious to get rid of me." His voice dropped to a deep murmur. "Not so fast. We have that other business."

Lauren's heart slammed against her chest once with the impact of his words and again with fear of them.

Yes, yes they did.

CHAPTER 10

Lauren had made herself scarce for the past couple of weeks since the planning board meeting. Sonja had said she was busy with that new project with her firm's biggest client. If Jesse didn't know better, he'd say his fearless Lauren was afraid of their attraction and what they were going to do about it. He bounded down the stairs. Or she really had moved on to break the tie that had bound them even when they'd ended things before. But what Lauren didn't know is that he'd moved on, too, leaving behind the rash racer he'd been as a younger man. He had the patience now to wait and find out for sure.

Without a conscious thought, he found himself humming "I'll Wait for You," their song. The bittersweet memories it evoked ran through his head. He raked his hand through his hair. Next thing he knew, he'd be picking up a few extra bucks writing a column for the lovelorn for the local paper. Not that he couldn't use the bucks.

Lauren's appearance at the other door stopped his steps. He'd learned patience, but only to a point. When they'd arrived home at the same time yesterday, it had hit him how much he'd missed her. So, he'd talked her into stopping by today to see the progress he and his dad had made, couching it as an inspection in case she ran into anyone from the planning board.

She opened her door.

"Hi," he said. "You're up and out early."

"I knew you usually leave about now."

So she kept track of his schedule. He tamped down the boost to his ego. She probably knew what time his father left, too. She did live right next door.

"And I have an early client meeting this morning." She walked onto the porch wearing one of what he thought of as her more lawerly suits. If her intent was to look business unisex, it didn't work on him, at least. Lauren was all woman, no matter how she might try to hide it.

"You can look at our work progress another day, if that would be better. The improvements will still be there."

She caught up with him on the slate walkway leading from the house. "Today's fine."

Was it, or did she just want to get the inspection, time with him over with? She *had* avoided him for two weeks, which had to have taken some effort considering they lived in the same building. What was with him? He didn't second guess things, and Lauren wasn't a person whose words had double meanings.

"I'll follow you over," she said, heading toward her car in the driveway while he continued down the walkway to his truck parked on the street.

He hopped into his truck, powered it on, and flicked the directional to pull out. The flash on the dashboard was like a light bulb going off. What was with him was that he wanted Lauren to cheer on his construction work like she used to cheer him on at races. His stomach clenched at his neediness. This love stuff was sick torture.

Jesse stopped at the mansion gate, got out of his truck, and unlocked the gate. He swung it open and walked back to her car. She rolled down her window.

"I'll pull in so you can get around my truck. Go ahead up to the house. I'm going to relock the gate." He paused. "What the planning board chair said about people trespassing and possibly getting hurt on the property."

Lauren nodded solemnly, but the corners of her lips twitched.

Jesse felt her gaze on his back as he walked to his truck and drove through the open gate. He needed to stop trying to impress Lauren and be himself, or it would be the death of him. Jesse waited in the truck while Lauren pulled around him and headed up the driveway. Then, he locked up and followed her, excitement building. Wait until Lauren saw what he and Dad had accomplished. He'd had trouble getting the foundation people scheduled until this week, so they'd done all the foundation prep they could and concentrated on the cottage, which was nearly done. They probably could move in this weekend and get one thing off his plate.

He pulled behind Lauren's car and exited his truck with a big grin on his face. A grin Lauren didn't return.

"I'm so sorry," she said.

Sorry for what? His gaze followed hers to the cottage. All the windows, his custom- ordered windows had been smashed. His breakfast settled like a dead weight in his stomach as he rushed to the door and unlocked it. As if he needed to with the tall living room windows busted out. He braced himself, but it wasn't enough to stop the bile rising. The damage inside in the living room was limited to graffiti on the newly painted walls. He should check the bedrooms and kitchen, but his work boots were rooted to the hardwood floor, which thankfully, hadn't been damaged.

Lauren stepped beside him and squeezed his hand with hers. "This time, you're calling the police."

He gave her a noncommittal grunt. "I need to check the kitchen and bedrooms."

Lauren tightened her hand on his, and that unrooted his feet. He blew out his pent-up breath when they entered the kitchen. No damage. "That leaves the bedrooms." He tugged Lauren along, his boost from the kitchen inspection sinking with each glimpse into the three rooms. The unpainted interiors were untouched, but the windows had been broken.

"I'd thought we'd move in this weekend," he said, as much to himself as to Lauren. He closed the last door and reassessed the living room.

"You still have two weeks to meet Judge Trexler and Child Service's deadline."

"All of the living room windows were custom-ordered and took a week to come in."

Lauren cocked her head to the side. "But you just need to replace the glass, don't you?"

Where was his head? He examined the window frames. She was right. They were fine. All he needed was a glazier to help him and Dad replace the glass. Jesse strode back and hugged Lauren.

"You're right." He rested his forehead against hers, resisting the pull to lower his lips and take solace in hers. "But Dad and would have to take time out of the other work to repair the cottage before we can I move in. And we only four weeks now to have the mansion stabilized, too. I couldn't find anyone that could start the foundation work before today."

Jesse lifted his head and Lauren stepped back. He glanced out the window. Speaking of the foundation work, the contractor should be showing up any minute with its equipment.

Lauren nodded. "Considering the circumstances, I see no problem with your provisional custody being extended until the structural work on the mansion is done and the cottage is repaired."

He knew that was supposed to reassure him, but it didn't. He didn't want anything to jeopardize his custody of Shelley. Jesse kicked an empty beer can the vandals must have left behind. "I'm supposed to take care of my family."

Lauren reached up and placed her finger to his lips. "You are to the best of your ability. That's one of the things I lo … admire about you."

Her word stumble and blush sent a shiver down his spine.

She dropped her hand to her side. "I've got to run."

Away from him, from what she'd started to say?

"That meeting. Call the police." Lauren's voice was all business now.

An army of emotions warred inside him as he watched her walk to her car. The problem with giving his best was that it never seemed to be good enough.

Officer Ben Andrews closed his pad. "This could be random vandalism. You're sure you can't think of anyone who might want to get back at you for something?"

"I haven't been here long enough to make any enemies," Jesse said.

"I'm only asking because you were a national figure on the motocross circuit. Anything from then?"

Had Ben emphasized *were*, or was he being overly sensitive? He had kind of liked the guy after he'd learned he was happily married, and that he and Lauren really were no more than friends. That is until he'd grilled him earlier on the insurance coverage on the property as if he'd done the damage himself for money.

"And I heard you recently got custody of your daughter," Ben said.

Jesse fisted his hands. From living with Mac and Dana in Chenango Falls as a teen when he first started racing, he knew how people tended to know everyone's business in a small place. But he didn't need Shelley dragged into this.

His dad, who'd been boarding up the back windows, came up behind him. Before Jesse could say anything, his dad faced off with Ben, looking every inch the custom bike shop owner he'd been. "I heard what you were saying to Jesse earlier about the insurance. We had the cottage all finished, ready for us to move in as the final step in Jesse having permanent custody of his daughter. He wouldn't have done anything to jeopardize that, no matter what the money."

Jesse uncurled his fingers and touched his father's arm. They'd had their differences in the past, but Jesse just realized something they had in common. A fierce protective love for the females in their family. Child and adult. His heart thumped, remembering his and his father's love for his mother and, then, what Lauren had almost said earlier—or what he thought she'd been about to say. Protective love for the women in their family *and* those they wanted to be part of their family.

"Mr. Brewster. I was only going to ask if Jesse had gotten any push back from his daughter's mother's family."

"No," Jesse answered. "My daughter's aunt, her only relative on record, dropped her off with nothing more than a suitcase and said she was my responsibility before speeding away, address unknown. Until then, I didn't even know she existed."

Ben lifted the plastic evidence bag with the beer can in it. "I'll take this back to the station and see if we can lift any fingerprints. Unless you can think of anything else that might help."

Jesse shook his head. "No."

Ben hesitated. "Is Lauren still your attorney?"

"Why? Do I need one?" Technically Lauren was until the name change was done. But Jesse was anxious to break that connection ASAP for a better one with her.

"No. Acer handled the property, the estate settlement. She might have some insight from that."

Jesse scuffed the toe of his work boot against the sandy ground. "Right." Lauren had pressed him hard to report the stolen and replaced gas. Which he hadn't.

"Did you tell him about the gas?" his father asked, as if reading his mind. More likely, he was still peeved about the insurance questions.

"What about gas?" Ben asked.

Jesse filled him in.

"I could have used this information sooner. Report anything else right away." Ben said.

"You'll keep us informed?" Jesse's father asked.

Ben nodded and strode to his patrol car.

Jesse surveyed the damage to the cottage again. "What am I going to do?" he asked more to himself than of his father.

"*We're* going to work harder and smarter," his dad answered.

Jesse patted his father's shoulder. He appreciated all Dad was doing. And the project and little Shelley had pulled his father back into life. But Jesse knew how tired he was at the end of their long days, and how worn out Dad looked in the evening. How much more could his father—and he admitted it, could he—give?

"That college kid Sonja recommended from church is starting tomorrow," his father reminded him.

"Yeah." The guy had good work recommendations, but no real experience in construction beyond helping his folks do some interior updates on their house.

"You could hire additional help."

Jesse hadn't shared how close he and Sonja were on financing. Shadows of his father's disappointment had stopped him. Disappointment when Jesse hadn't wanted to be an engineer, as his father had hoped; when he'd chosen racing; when he'd dropped his part-time college classes as he became more successful on the circuit. He rolled his lips in and out. Then, of course, there was his accident.

"I'll talk with Sonja."

"Yeah, you need to let her know."

The sounds of large equipment filled the silence that had opened between them. The foundation crew.

"Go ahead, make your call," his father said. "I'll handle things with the contractor."

"Thanks, Dad." For a whole lot more than today. Jesse's chest tightened. He was getting maudlin now. Or it could be apprehension about calling Sonja, about old patterns repeating themselves. Jesse paced in front of the cottage while the phone rang.

"Hi, Jesse, you just caught me," Sonja answered. "I'm on my way out to a showing, a second showing."

Sonja's confident enthusiasm reminded him of Lauren when she got all bubbly about something she was excited about. Or how Lauren used to get all bubbly. He hadn't seen much of that side of Lauren since he'd arrived in Indigo Bay. He shook his head as if that could clear the cloud that had descended on him when he saw the damage to the cottage.

"The foundation people didn't reschedule again, did they?" she asked. "They know our time frame."

"No, they're here." He paused. "Someone vandalized the cottage. Shelley and I aren't going to be able to move in this week." Jesse continued over the squawk of dismay from Sonja. "Dad and I are going to have to move on to the big house and come back to the cottage repairs, if we're going to make the planning board deadline. We may have to hire some more help." He might as well get that out front.

"You have to do what you have to do. I can take a loan against my retirement account if needed to cover the costs. And I know someone I can recommend for the work, part-time, at least. His name is Jace Fisher. But Jace's part-time would be as good or better than someone less experienced full time."

Jesse tried not to give into the relief that washed over him. "Thanks, but I don't want you overextending yourself for me."

"Get this right. It's not for you. It's for me. The B&B is *my* dream business. I've got two showings today. I can't get over until late afternoon to see the damage. You called the police?"

"Yes, and there's no need to come over. I can tell you tonight."

"My prospective buyers are here. Lauren can come look at the damage for me."

He hadn't told her Lauren had already seen it. Jesse had too many emotions tangled up in that meeting right now.

"She's our attorney, after all," Sonja said. "And I'll text you Jace's contact information." Sonja clicked off.

Jesse stared at the blank phone screen. He didn't know what Lauren being their attorney—and his only until Shelley's last name change was final—had to do with the vandalism. What he did know is that he didn't need Lauren witnessing his life falling apart again.

~

"Brittany, I'll be out for a while," Lauren said. Hey, Ray and Gerry did it all of the time. They were both out now. She'd make it up to Brittany another time for leaving her to handle the office alone.

"Early lunch?" Brittany asked.

"Client meeting," Lauren answered before her co-worker could ask her to pick-up something. "I'm not sure how long I'll be gone."

Brittany's knowing look as Lauren exited the office said she knew exactly which client, too. Of course, that wasn't hard. Lauren had only a few clients with open business right now and Jesse and Ken Kostner were the only male ones. Ken had been her early morning appointment. She'd jumped into his project, even though she was technically still working with Jesse. But not for long. She'd gotten notice this morning of the hearing for Shelley's name change, which for all practical purposes was just a formality. But that wasn't the only reason she was on her way back to the mansion to see Jesse. *No.* It was her mother's phone call a few minutes ago. Mom had let it drop that she was tapping into her retirement account to hire more workers to stay on schedule with the renovations, despite the vandalism.

A salty tang in the air made Lauren glance at the sky before she got into her car. The darkening clouds rolling in signaled a coastal storm. A storm that couldn't match the one she'd start if she tried to advise her mother against borrowing against her retirement funds.

She needed to talk to Jesse without her mother, see how deep he and her mother were getting in and with what, or whom. The uneasiness that plagued her about the project erupted again. Indigo Bay didn't see much truly destructive vandalism. And it had bothered her that Ken had asked about the B&B project this morning and said his offer for the property still stood.

It was pouring rain when Lauren pulled up to the cottage. The site looked deserted, except for some excavating equipment. As she was debating whether to make a dash for the cottage or leave, Jesse came out of the building holding a square of plywood over his head, taking the chill off the day. Her knight in shining armor.

He opened the car door for her. "Your mother called to warn me you might be on your way, although I didn't clearly pick up on why. I don't know what impression you got earlier or from talking to your mother, but you didn't need to come back."

She stepped out under the board, close to him. He didn't want her here? Her heart sank. That wasn't the impression she'd gotten earlier. *Too bad.* From the professional side, she was still his lawyer, for now at least. As for the relationship side, who knew what they were doing?

"But I'm glad you did come by."

Once inside the cottage, her heart dropped again at the wall graffiti and the now boarded up windows.

"Oh, Jesse." She touched his arm as he straightened from leaning the piece of plywood against the wall.

"It's not that bad. I have this under control, although it means we have to postpone moving from your mother's place. On the plus side, the foundation equipment and crew arrived today and we have them working exclusively here until the job is done."

"Assuming the weather clears," Lauren said.

A muscle in his jaw twitched.

Why had she said that?

His expression remained sober. "What are the chances I could get an extension on the rehabilitation agreement if the weather does cause further delay?"

"The board might consider it if we have a stretch of inclement weather." She hesitated. She had to be straight with Jesse. "The vandalism probably works against you. That someone was able to get onto the property and do the damage supports the city's concern about someone getting hurt in the condemned mansion."

Jesse dropped his chin to his chest in a familiar action she'd seen many times when he was racing. He'd finish a race, whip off his helmet and look at his time. If it wasn't what he wanted, expected, he'd drop his head for an on the spot analysis of what he'd done wrong.

"I shouldn't have spent the time on the cottage first. It doesn't matter much if Social Services supervises my guardianship for a while longer. Your mother is fine with us staying with her. Maybe more than fine, where my dad's involved."

The quirk of his lips when he mentioned her mom and his dad was a magnet. She stepped closer. "But you couldn't get any excavation company scheduled to shore up the foundation until today. That could work to your advantage." She shivered with a wave of uneasiness. For a plum job like this, she was surprised he hadn't had local companies falling over each other to start the job. There wasn't that much new construction going on in Indigo Bay.

"Cold?" he asked. Not waiting for an answer, he closed the steps between them and wrapped his warm, strong arms around her.

"No." Her shiver played into the conspiracy thoughts she had no basis for. She didn't want to think. She just wanted to feel. Lauren wrapped her arms around Jesse's neck and pulled his lips to hers.

After a moment's hesitation, he accepted her offering and made her one back, capturing her lips with a kiss that was soft and demanding at the same time. Too soon he pulled back with a dazed look on his face.

"I love you, still, again, when I have nothing to offer you." His lips moved in words she wasn't sure she was supposed to hear.

His bemusement was replaced with an expression she wasn't used to seeing on his face—defeat.

"I think …"

Jesse's cell phone rang.

Lauren ignored it and his further pull back. "I think I'm falling back in love with you, too."

The phone rang again, and he frowned as he drew it from his pocket.

She shouldn't have been so tentative. The truth was she loved Jesse more than ever, as a woman, not a girl. He had so much to offer that had nothing to do with his financial worth.

"Brewster," he said into the phone, listening to what whoever on the other end was saying. "Yeah, thanks for the update."

Jesse shoved the phone in his back pocket. "That was Ben. They've got a kid for the damage."

Nothing of the potentially life changing moment they'd shared showed in Jesse, except in the stiff way he held himself. But that could mean anything.

"That was fast," she said, controlling her voice to be as bland as his had been as she reined in her racing heart.

"There was a beer can. It had a fingerprint on it. Ben said they connected it to a local kid who'd been picked up last months for underage drinking."

"Oh." That was still quick work. Lauren noticed the drum of rain on the roof had stopped. "Sounds like the rain has stopped. I should get back to the office. I'll swing by and get you a copy of the police report from Ben."

"Sure," Jesse said.

That was it? Lauren pushed open the cottage door. The angry thunderclouds still obliterated the sun. But the rain had stopped, unlike the storm their kiss had started inside her. She dashed for her car, leaving without accomplishing what she'd come to do—talk with Jesse about the project and her mother's financial backing and tell him about the name change hearing.

Jesse, being close to Jesse, had messed with her organized thoughts, as had happened too often since they day they met. She touched her fingertip to her lips. He'd said he loved her. But, again, he wasn't going to let himself accept the reality of that love until he proved whatever it was he thought he had to prove to her.

Lauren had pulled herself together by the time she entered the police station.

"Hi," Ben said. "Let me guess. You've come for a copy of the Brewster vandalism report."

"Yep. You sure got to the bottom of that fast."

Ben looked from side to side. "The Chief made it a priority," he said in a low voice. "He, most of us, are anxious to see the mansion restored. It's part of Indigo Bay's history."

Lauren took the sheaf of papers Ben handed her.

"The case isn't solved yet. The kid said he was hired to vandalize the property through an online ad."

CHAPTER 11

*U*nbelievable. Just when everything had been falling back into place. The rain had set them back almost another week on the foundation work. But once that was done, with Jace Fisher's help and another local Jace recommended, they had worked like wildfire the last two weeks on the other mansion repairs. Jesse spat. *Yeah, wildfire.*

He raised his eyes to the fire department trucks dousing the last of the flames from the fire that had nearly engulfed the back rooms of the mansion.

The fire inspector and chief and Ben approached him.

"What's the word?" Jesse asked.

"Almost without a doubt arson," the inspector said.

"Damages?"

"Extensive. They may impact the structural integrity."

"Making the property condemnable again." Jesse uttered an expletive. There was no way his small crew could rectify the fire damage and complete the interim requirements of the agreement with the planning board in the four days they had left.

The inspector looked him in the eye, and Jesse recognized him from the planning board. It made sense the inspector would sit on the board.

"I'm afraid so. Sad," the man mused. "A beautiful old building like this. Son, maybe if you hadn't ditched the first condemnation meeting, you wouldn't have gotten into the time crunch you did."

But he hadn't ditched the meeting, had he? No, he or Dad would have known if the letter about the meeting had arrived at his parents' house.

"I'll be back when it's cooled to finish my inspection," the inspector said.

"My guys will be heading out, too," the fire chief said.

That left him and Ben standing in the early morning sun.

"I'll need to take another statement," Ben said. "Do you want to call Lauren?"

"Why? Because you and the inspector think I set the fire?"

Ben's eyes narrowed. "No, because she and you … I know my first call would be to my wife Eva."

"Sorry, man. You're right." Jesse pulled out his phone and stopped before he pressed Lauren's number. Lauren wasn't his lawyer anymore. After the hearing on Shelley's name change last week, Lauren had said she couldn't represent him at the final planning board meeting because Acer and Acer were contracted to cover for the city attorney while he was on vacation. It would be a conflict of interest. She'd said that since the work on the property would be done, the board review would be a formality, and had given him the name of another lawyer in Indigo Bay. Jesse kicked a stone. He'd never called the guy.

"Could I come over to the station in an hour or so for that report?" Jesse asked. "I want to look around here first."

"As long as the firefighters are still here and you honor the crime scene tape."

"I won't tamper with evidence," he said, unable to keep the sarcastic tone from his voice."

"Dave," Ben shouted to the fire chief's retreating back. "Can you stick around? Brewster wants to see the damage. I'm heading back to the station."

"Yeah," he answered. "I should keep one of the trucks here a while longer to make sure there are no more flare ups."

"I'll see you in an hour," Ben said.

"Right." Jesse trudged to the back of the structure. He didn't really want to see the damage. What he wanted was to recapture the moment he and Lauren had had at the cottage before he'd jumped the gun and blurted that he loved her. He hadn't seen her alone since, and when she'd given him the other lawyer's name and number, he'd felt like she was cutting him loose. He surveyed the charred water-logged building, unsure he had the reserves to fight for both Lauren and his inheritance. But without his inheritance, could he justify even asking Lauren to give him another chance?

"Hey, did you hear about the fire at the Morrison—I mean, Brewster—mansion?"

Lauren stopped dead in front of Brittany's desk in the firm's reception area. "No. How? What?"

"My friend's boyfriend is a volunteer firefighter."

That wasn't exactly the how and what she'd been referring to.

"Wicked damage," Brittany said.

Lauren's throat tightened. "Mom said they were so close to finished with the required structural repairs."

"Pardon?"

"Jesse had the project on schedule. He was all set for the interim review meeting with the planning board set for this Thursday."

"What happens …" Brittany's phone rang. "Yeah, she just walked in. I'll tell her." Brittany hung up the phone. "Ray wants to see you."

Lauren dragged her feet to her boss's office. She needed to call Jesse.

"Sit, please," Ray said.

That second cup of coffee she'd gulped down before leaving home sloshed in her stomach.

"Do you have that corporate filing for Ken Kostner done?"

The churning subsided. "Yes." But Ray could have checked that himself.

"Good. Going forward, he'll be using his new partner's attorney in Charleston."

Lauren swallowed hard. Kostner was their biggest client. Was Ray giving her notice? She and Jesse would both be unemployed. She restrained the humorless laugh that bubbled up, so that it came out as more of a choking sound.

"Was it something I did. Ken leaving?"

Ray leaned back in his chair. "No, not at all. Ken and I go way back, but he's been dabbling in some things I'd rather not have the firm associated with."

A dam inside her broke loose. "Then, the firm really didn't receive the notice of the first condemnation hearing for the old Morrison property. You haven't been helping Ken try to convince Jesse to sell the mansion property?" *Convince* was the polite word, considering what she suspected Kostner might be doing.

"No, we didn't get the notice, and what are you talking about?"

"Talk I heard." From her internal voices.

"I hope you quashed any connection to the firm."

"I did." Lauren's face pinked. *By keeping my suspicions to myself.* Relief that she had kept quiet, loosened her taut muscles a millimeter.

Ray frowned. "The other reason we need to talk is the planning board meeting on Thursday."

He must have heard about the fire.

"You're going to have to cover for me."

Ray's words squeezed all the air from her lungs.

"Gerry's on vacation and I have this stent thing I have to have done tomorrow morning at the hospital. It's no big deal. The meeting, that is. Your mother said most of the required work was completed last weekend. It'll be a routine approval."

He hadn't heard about the fire.

Ray patted her hand across the desk. "Don't look so worried, the doc says the surgery is no big deal either."

"I'm glad to hear that." *But that's not what I'm worried about. If the board won't extend Jesse's project deadline, I'll be helping to take his dream away from him.* "But about the meeting. The city may want to get another law firm. Conflict of interest with me having represent Jesse at the original meeting."

"No, with Kostner leaving, we need to keep the city happy and keep the contract we have with it. Besides it will be a slam dunk."

"Right."

"Was there something else?" Ray asked when she made no move to rise from the chair.

The fire. "No, just my thoughts for a speedy recovery from your surgery."

"Thanks. I'm taking the rest of the day off. You should swing by city hall and pick up any additional information you'll need for the planning board meeting."

"Yeah, I'll do that." Lauren rose and walked to her office. She pulled out her cell phone to call Jesse. *No.* She'd call her mother. She wasn't ready to talk with Jesse.

"Hey, Mom. What's the damage?" she asked, assuming Jesse would have called her mother and getting right to the point.

"It doesn't look good. Jesse said the fire inspector thinks there's structural damage and, even if there isn't, Jesse doesn't see any way we're going to be able to meet the renovation contract deadline, unless you can get us an extension. We'll have the fire insurance reimbursement to work with."

Lauren clutched her phone. "I can't do that, Mom. I'm not Jesse's attorney anymore, and I can't represent you on this, either. Acer and Acer are representing

Indigo Bay through the end of this month while the city attorney is on vacation. I have to handle the planning board meeting because Gerry is also on vacation and Ray is having surgery. It's my job."

"Oh."

Her mother's subdued voice took Lauren back to the years between her father's leaving them and her mother finding herself in Indigo Bay. The years when she took care of Mom financially and emotionally, while trying to finish college, when Jesse let her push him away to do so because he was so wrapped up in racing. It was a place she didn't want to be, but didn't see a choice. She had to live her life.

"Do you want me to tell Jesse?" her mother said into the silence.

"No, I'll call him." *Just not yet.* Lauren clicked off, turned around and walked back out of her office. "I'm heading out to city hall," she said to Brittany over her shoulder as she let the office door close behind her.

"Lauren, wait up," Jesse called as she approached the city hall steps.

She turned and waited. What else could she do.

"Have you talked with your mother?"

"Yes."

"Then you know about the fire, the damage. I'm on my way in to get the paperwork to file for an extension with the board. What do you think our chances are?"

"Your chances? I don't want to speculate." *Because she didn't want to tell him, probably not good.*

"Any advice about the extension application?" Jesse's voice was strained.

"Sorry. I shouldn't. I'm not your attorney anymore."

His eyes narrowed at her correction. "The conflict of interest. Acer being the city attorney's back up. Come on." Jesse's impatience showed in his wide legged stance. "It's not like you'll be representing the city at the board meeting."

"It's exactly like that." Lauren explained the situation. "And I don't know about an extension. The mess up about the first condemnation hearing will weigh against you."

"You, too?" he spat.

Lauren had no idea what he was talking about. "It's my job."

"There are other jobs."

He couldn't want her to walk out on her job.

"You haven't been completely happy with it," he went on.

He did want her to.

"What about us?" he asked.

That plea that tore at her heart. She steeled herself. "If there's going to be an us, one of us needs to have a job."

"Yeah, and that couldn't possibly be me. Forget it. I'm going in for the application, futile as it may be."

"Jesse, it's not. I didn't …"

He strode up the stairs and into the building. She followed and hid out in the Ladies Room until he'd had enough time to get his application from the city clerk.

"Hey Lauren," the city clerk said. "You just missed Jesse. Sad about the mansion, the fire."

"Yes." But not as sad as what it was doing to the relationship that had been growing between her and

Jesse. Correct that. What she was doing to their relationship.

"I hope he gets his extension. I was going to call you. I have some information that might help you and Jesse with the extension application."

The clerk must think she was still Jesse's attorney. Lauren made a snap decision. She could listen to what the clerk had to say, and ask Brittany to call and request the mansion files be sent over to the office later.

"What's that?" she asked.

"There was an inquiry about buying the mansion property at the city's condemned valuation from a company I'd never heard of before. Bayside Vacation Getaways."

Lauren went cold. The incorporation she'd recently filed for Ken Kostner and his new partner.

"It was like the company didn't know Jesse still owned the property, thought the city had taken it as eminent domain. And I found something in the bottom of a file drawer that you'll want to see." The clerk reached under the counter for a file folder she handed Lauren.

Lauren opened it and gazed wide-eyed at the contents. "The planning board has this information?"

"No, only the city attorney's office."

Lauren gripped the folder to stop herself from a fist-pump *yes*. "I'll look into it and advise the board."

Yes, she needed to fulfill her promise to herself, but that didn't mean she couldn't help Jesse or that there wasn't room in her life for him and Shelley, too.

Jesse and his father walked into the meeting room Thursday night for the planning board meeting. He hadn't bothered calling the lawyer Lauren had recommended. He'd spent enough of Sonja's money already. And for all the support she'd given him, Sonja called him this morning to tell him about an inquiry she'd had about the property, if he needed a contingency plan. An offer he was ready to take if the board denied his extension request.

The offer wasn't enough to start the bike shop he wanted to open with Dad, but, along with the fire insurance proceeds, it would enough to pay Sonja back the money she'd fronted him and finance a nest egg for the shop. He could rent a place for him and Shelley and Dad, too. That is, if they decided to stay here, or if he did. Dad might choose to stay in Indigo Bay whether he and Shelley did or not because of Sonja. Jesse gripped the folder with his copy of the extension application. Lauren wasn't the only one who could provide for them. He was a top-notch mechanic who could get work almost anywhere. It might not be the future his father had envisioned for him, but it was honest work that he could enjoy. Work that could keep his dream of a life with Lauren alive. That is if Lauren wanted a life with him.

The two men made their way to the front of the spectator-filled room. Dallas and the other board members nodded to them from the dais, except for Bill Crowley. He smiled, sending a chill down Jesse's spine. Lauren hadn't arrived yet. He rubbed the back of his neck. Avoiding him as she had since he'd run into her at city hall on Monday? He'd texted her an apology of sorts that afternoon and received a terse response that she couldn't speak to him until after this meeting.

Dallas glanced at the wall clock behind him. It looked like he was wondering where Lauren was, too. "We can get started folks, as soon as the city attorney arrives."

As if that was her cue, Lauren rushed in with Ben, briefcase swinging. "Sorry, we're late. The police department was waiting for some information pertinent to this meeting."

"This meeting of the Indigo Bay Planning Board is called to order." Dallas presented the facts of the rehabilitation agreement and the application for extension. "Mr. Brewster."

Jesse rose to a frown from Lauren. Probably because he hadn't hired her lawyer friend. He cleared his throat. "I think Mr. Harper's summation of my application accurately presents Sonja and my vision for my great uncle's property and how it fits and will benefit Indigo Bay, as well as the unforeseen obstacles we've run into."

Lauren's frown deepened.

Facts were facts. Jesse didn't see any benefit in belaboring them.

"Thank you, Mr. Brewster. Now, I'll open the meeting to comments from the public with a follow up from the board, unless the city attorney wants to start with the information she has?"

Lauren glanced at Bill. "No, I'll defer to later."

Jesse's stomach burned. What was she up to? Bailing out her mother as she'd had to in the past. Didn't she realize that Sonja didn't need or want that from her anymore?

"All right," Dallas said, "anyone who has a comment, please line up at the microphone."

Jesse gulped as the line ran the length of the room and out into the hall. Maybe people were this civically active in a small place like Indigo Bay. He checked out the surprised looks on some of the board members faces and the self-satisfied one on Bill's. Either that or he was the dead man he'd feared he was when he'd walked in. After all, he was an outsider. Lauren's expression was neutral.

The first person to the mic was the city clerk. "I think the board should grant the extension." She went on about the historic value of the mansion and the role it and the Morrisons had played in the founding and growth of Indigo Bay. "I don't know Mr. Brewster that well, but I do know Sonja Cooper, and I think you have to agree that she's been an asset to Indigo Bay since she moved here."

A man Jesse didn't recognize stepped up with a comment that Indigo Bay needed to become less insular if it wanted to grow and prosper in the 21st century and that a large resort would be a way to do that. Caroline Harper followed him with comments similar to the city clerk's and outlining the vandalism and weather delays the project had suffered. And so it went, with people he recognized supporting his extension alternating with people he, for the most part, didn't recognize opposing it. About half-way through the line, Jesse picked up on Bill nodding to most of the opposition as if thanking them. He squirmed in his chair. Were they ringers? *Nah.* He'd read one too many John Grishom books.

"Ms. Cooper, Officer Andrews," Dallas invited them to the mic."

"We'll defer to the board," she said.

Jesse locked his gaze with hers and a rush rocketed through him when he caught the glint in her eyes. She *was* up to something, and if he had to place a bet, he'd bet on something in his favor. The rush was replaced with warmth.

"Anything from the board?" Dallas asked.

"Yes," Bill shot out before Dallas had finished. "All the sentiment voiced here tonight is fine and good. But from an objective financial standpoint, the Morrison property has better uses than as a bed and breakfast. Uses that can bring in more money, employ more people."

"Money for him, most likely," someone behind Jesse muttered.

"And," Bill continued, "we have to ask, how well do we know Jesse Brewster or Sonja Cooper, and how well do they know us and what's good for Indigo Bay? He's from California. She's from New York."

That comment got some nods from the board and other people in the room.

"If Mr. Brewster was so all fired up to rescue his inheritance from condemnation, why did he blow off the original condemnation meeting, after receiving the notice? His signoff to the registered letter is in the city clerk's file. I think he's had plenty of time to come here and renovate if he was serious about doing it."

Jesse fisted and loosened his fingers as a hum of murmurs ran through the room and his earlier optimism dissipated.

"Then, there's the vandalism and arson. My understanding is that the insurance company hasn't paid on the damages yet. Maybe it wasn't vandalism and arson?"

Bill's implied accusation made Jesse push back in his seat to stand. His father touched his arm, killing Jesse's inclination to march up and punch Bill's smug look off his face.

"That's all." Bill brushed his palms against each other as if washing himself of the whole thing.

"Ms. Cooper, Officer Andrews. Want to take the mic now?"

Jesse couldn't tell if Dallas' strident tone was because of Bill's comments or impatience with whatever Lauren and Ben were up to.

"I will," Lauren said. She stepped up to the dais and passed out sheets to the board members before taking the mic Dallas had been using. "As you can see from the report I've provided, Mr. Brewster did not receive notice of the first condemnation hearing. Because of the sensitive nature of the information, as the acting city attorney, I advise the board go into executive session before we continue."

Jesse felt the crowd's gasp tenfold. It appeared Lauren was using her position as acting city attorney for, not against, him, as well as protecting the city.

"We could have done without the drama, Ms. Cooper," Dallas said, glancing at the report. "But the board will take your advice and go into executive session. Everyone, except the board, Mr. Brewster, Ms. Cooper, and Officer Andrews, please clear the room. If you want to stay outside the room for our vote after the session, someone will notify you when you can return."

"Good luck, son," Jesse's father said as he passed behind him to follow out with the others.

Once the door had closed behind the last person to leave, Dallas said, "Ms. Cooper you may want to enlighten Mr. Brewster with your report, assuming you have not."

"I have not." She took the three steps to the table.

Her hand brushed his seemingly on purpose as she handed him the report. But he'd misread things like that before.

"I wanted to tell you. I truly did," she said for his ears only. But as acting city attorney, I couldn't." Lauren straightened and went back to the mic.

Jesse's gut twisted and his heart pounded. He couldn't tell from her ambiguous words whether she planned to help or hurt his cause. And the way her light summer suit skimmed her curves, didn't help the push pull of his hope and doubt.

"As you can see," she said. "Jesse, Mr. Brewster's, signature on the registered letter return card doesn't match the signatures on either the rehabilitation contract or his extension application. We've had an expert verify that the signatures are, indeed, different. Also, the return card does not have the post office's cancelled stamp on it."

"That doesn't prove he didn't get the condemnation notice," Bill interrupted. "Maybe someone in the clerk's office lost the original card, got another from the Post Office and faked it." He sat back and crossed his arms.

"Close," Lauren said. "The notice was prepared to go out during the month property taxes are due. The city hires on temporary workers to help with the collection and paperwork. One of the temps was handling mail runs. As far as the city clerk, Ben, and I have found, the notice was never sent. The city doesn't have any charge or receipt for the notice mailing cost. Whether the notice not getting in the mail was accidental—Lauren looked at Bill—or deliberate, we may never know for sure."

Bill uncrossed his arms and leaned on the dais. "That doesn't dismiss the suspicions Brewster damaged his own property for the insurance money."

"Suspicions only you may hold," Lauren said.

Dallas cleared his throat.

"I'll let Officer Andrews fill you all in on that."

Ben rose and spoke from his seat. "My department has learned that the vandalism and arson were definitely just that. The perpetrators were paid to cause the damage. Payments we've traced to a company named Bayside Vacation Getaways."

Bill blanched.

"Ah, Bill, I thought you might have heard of it, since you're an investor in it."

The room went silent.

"That property," Bill sputtered, "is worth a fortune. You're all fools to block Bayside from building the exclusive resort we want on it."

"Enough." Dallas said.

"If you can take your vote without him," Ben said, "I'd like Mr. Crowley to come with me to the station to answer some questions."

"Sure," Dallas said. "You can let the public back in for our vote on your way out."

Jesse slumped in his seat. His girl, no his woman, his annoying, wonderful Lauren had done it. She'd risked her job, her security, for him. And he was going to prove himself worthy of her every day of the rest of his life if she'd let him.

"Hey, mister, need a lift?" Lauren asked when she caught up with Jesse outside city hall searching the street for Dad and his truck.

"It looks like I might," he said with a wry smile. "Can't find Dad. His truck is gone."

Lauren smiled. "All I know is that I texted him when the vote on your extension hit the third yes vote needed for approval to say you had another ride home."

"You were magnificent in there."

She shrugged. "I don't know about that. I was doing my job."

"More like you were risking your job for me."

"Nothing that noble. You were going to sell out your dream. Mom told me about the offer from Bayside. I simply did what was best for you, for the city, and for the firm. For everyone."

"Everyone? Even yourself?" He draped his arm around her shoulders.

She leaned into him feeling his solid support as they walked toward her car. "Especially for myself. You complete me. I'm not about to let you get away a third time, Jesse Brewster." She pressed her key fob to unlock the car. The warm evening air turned cool against her side when he released her to climb in the car.

"Lauren." Jesse's face had become the epitome of seriousness. "I can't survive losing you again."

She touched her forefinger to his lips. The lips she longed to have pressed to hers. "Wait. I'm taking you someplace where we can talk and stuff."

He squeezed her knee. "Stuff. I like the sounds of stuff."

She playfully swatted him way. "Behave, or there'll be no stuff." She drove past the city limits to a secluded bluff overlooking the ocean sunset.

"Am I allowed to talk now?" he asked as soon as she'd shut off the car. "You planned this just like you planned the trap for Bill at the board meeting."

She laughed. Jesse could always make her laugh. "Yes. Let me get the blanket I put in the back, and we can sit on the bluff and watch the sunset.

Jesse sat close to Lauren on the blanket and gazed out over the ocean. "It's beautiful. The ocean, the colors in the sky. But not as beautiful as you are. Inside and out." He turned in the seat to face her full on. "I love you so much."

"I love you, too, Jesse, with my whole heart."

He engulfed her hand in his, his work callused fingers a contrast to her more pampered one. "I don't know what I did to deserve that love, but I'm taking it and never letting go again."

"You'd better not." Her heart tripped just looking at his profile. Lauren slid her hand around the back of

Jesse's neck and pulled him toward her. She pressed her lips to his and closed her eyes to a kaleidoscope of colors as vivid as the sunset. Too soon for her, Jesse pulled back.

"I have a ring." Jesse looked as dazed as she felt. "Will you wear it? I bought it before my accident, when you were in college. We can exchange it if you don't like it."

The joy inside her bubbled out as a laugh. "Are you asking me to marry you?" She didn't wait for his answer. "If so, the answer is yes."

"Whoo-hoo!" Jesse pulled her into his arms, and brushed Lauren's hair back from her face. "That's my girl," he whispered before treating her to a deal-sealing kiss so full of the promise of love that it suspended all time.

EPILOGUE

Jesse stood at the back of the Beachside Chapel, Sonja's arm linked through his as three-and-a-half-year-old Shelly began her stroll down the aisle tossing rose petals right and left. His gaze at the altar caught Lauren's. She smiled and inclined her head toward his dad. He appeared to be in a daze fixated on his wife-to-be, unconsciously shifting his weight from foot to foot. Jesse shot back to last fall, when that was him standing up front waiting for his bride. He nearly stumbled with the love that overwhelmed him for Lauren, Shelley, his dad and Sonja.

"Hey," Sonja said. "I'm the one who's supposed to have jitters."

"But you don't."

"Not at all, but I can't say the same for Jeff."

"He'll be fine."

"I know."

The flash of a cell phone brought Jesse's attention to the people, their friends, they were passing: Lauren's law partners Ray and Gerry and their wives, the guys from his and Dad's bike shop, Shelley's preschool teacher and her husband, Caroline, Dallas, Jace, Ben and Eva, Lucille—who no doubt had Princess in her large bag—and countless others filling the pews. Everyone who'd helped them become part of the Indigo Bay community.

Jesse gave Sonja's hand to his father and took his place next to Lauren, resting his hand around her waist and smiling at the way her hand rested on her barely showing baby bump.

"Friends and family, we are gathered together today to …" the minister began the ceremony. "And I now pronounce you husband and wife. You may kiss your bride."

"Daddy, Mommy!" Shelley pulled on his coattail. "You said it was over when Pa kisses Grammy. Do I get cake now?"

A chuckle ran through the chapel.

But Jesse stood stock still for a moment before looking at Lauren. "She called me Daddy, not Jesse-Daddy," he whispered.

"And she called me Mommy, not Ren." Lauren looked as gut-struck as he felt.

"Yes." Jesse gazed at his wife and daughter. "We can go have cake now."

He squeezed Lauren tight to one side and Shelly to the other. Not that he needed cake. His life was pretty darn sweet already.

WHAT COMES NEXT?

Thank you for reading my story. I hope you enjoyed it and all the other Indigo Bay stories you've read.

And I always appreciate when my readers take the time to leave an honest review of my books.

If you're ready to spend more time in Indigo Bay, we have stories for you to read! Here's a list of all the stories in the Indigo Bay series. All of the stories are standalone and can be read in any order.

S P R I N G   2 0 1 9

Look for Jeff and Sonja's story in Sweet Horizons, Book 3 in the new Indigo Bay Second Chance Romances Series

Sweet Troublemaker by Jean Oram
Sweet Do-Over by Melissa McClone
Sweet Horizons by Jean C. Gordon
Sweet Whispers by Jeanette Lewis
Sweet Complications by Stacy Claflin
Sweet Adventure by Tamie Dearen

S P R I N G   2 0 1 8

Sweet Saturday by Pamela Kelley
Sweet Beginnings by Melissa McClone
Sweet Starlight by Kay Correll
Sweet Forgiveness by Jean Oram
Sweet Reunion by Stacy Claflin
Sweet Entanglement by Jean C. Gordon

D E C E M B E R   2 0 1 7

Sweet Holiday Surprise by Jean Oram
Sweet Holiday Memories by Kay Correll
Sweet Holiday Wishes by Melissa McClone
Sweet Holiday Traditions by Danielle Stewart

SPRING 2017

Sweet Dreams by Stacy Claflin
Sweet Matchmaker by Jean Oram
Sweet Sunrise by Kay Correll
Sweet Illusions by Jeanette Lewis
Sweet Regrets by Jennifer Peel
Sweet Rendezvous by Danelle Stewart

Find them all at http://sweetreadbooks.com/indigo-bay/.

TEAM MACACHEK
STARTS HERE

If you've enjoyed Jesse and Laura's story, read where it all began in this excerpt from *Mending the Motocross Champion*, available at popular online vendors and by order at your favorite bookstore.

EXCERPT FROM MENDING
THE MOTOCROSS CHAMPION

CHAPTER 1

The shrill of the phone woke her to her worst nightmare.

"Hello," the voice on the other end of the phone said. "This is Officer Conrad of the Pennsylvania State Police. May I speak to Dana Macachek?"

Her heart raced. No one had called her Dana Macachek in years.

"This is she."

"There's been an accident. Your husband Anton Macachek . . ."

No, no, no. Dana VanAlstyne gripped the edge of the bed stand for support as the words in her head momentarily drowned out the rest of what the officer was saying. An old, too familiar fear filled her, dredged from a part of her life she'd worked hard to put behind her.

". . . has been in an accident."

Ex-husband, Dana wanted to scream, as if that would take away the pain. Mac is my *ex-husband*. She sat up, swung her legs over the side of the bed, and cradled her head in her hand, the phone tight to her ear. Tears pricked her eyes.

"Is he all right?" she managed to get out in an almost reasonable sounding voice. Of course, he wasn't all right, or why would the officer be calling?

"He was sent by ambulance to Bucks Memorial Hospital."

"Then he's not . . ." She couldn't finish the sentence.

"He was alive at the scene."

"What happened?" she croaked.

"This is still a preliminary investigation. Apparently, he lost control of his SUV on an icy road sometime last night. Another driver came along early this morning and saw the vehicle and trailer off the road."

So he wasn't racing. Somehow, that calmed her. But he was the current U.S. motocross champion. Any other man in his position would have been flying, probably in a private jet. Or, at least traveling in a customized motor coach.

"Mrs. Macachek?"

"Yes, I'm here. How, how did you get my number?" She had to ask. It had been so long.

"Your husband had a card in his belongings listing you as next of kin in case of emergency."

"My ex-husband," she corrected. Wasn't that just like Mac to still have her listed as next of kin? Surely, he had friends who were closer to him now than she was.

Silence hung between them like dead air before a storm.

"Should I contact someone else?" the officer asked, impatience creeping into his voice.

The phone went silent as the officer waited for her to respond. Dana swallowed hard. She didn't know what to say, who the officer should call. Mac had no family left that she knew of.

Despite the shock and her concern, Dana couldn't stop the feeling of failure that washed over her. Although her mind was resigned to her divorce—they'd been so young—she'd never accepted her failure to keep her vows to Mac.

"No, no one else," she said in a voice that echoed calm and distant in her ears. "Can you give me directions to the hospital?"

"Where will you be coming from?"

"Chenango Falls, New York, north of Binghamton." Dana got up and walked over to the counter for the pen and pad she kept by the phone charger.

The officer gave her the directions.

"Thank you." Dana clicked off the phone and put her head down on the counter.

"Please," she prayed out loud, "please watch over Mac and keep him safe and—" Her voice broke. "And alive until I get there."

As soon as she could muster enough strength to stand, Dana went and threw a few things in a backpack. Thank goodness, it was Saturday and she didn't have to explain to anyone where she was going or that it involved Mac. Explanations could come later if she didn't make it into work on Monday.

She zipped the pack shut. The clinic could manage a day without her, even on short notice. That might be the one advantage of working for the Chenango Health Network, rather than having her own physical therapy practice. If she didn't come in, other people could cover for her. Her friend Sari would handle the church coffee hour tomorrow, too, if she had to stay over. Dana hated to dump her commitments on others, but the thought of Mac all alone chilled her. Despite everything that had passed between them, she had to know he was all right.

Four hours and two hundred miles later, Dana pulled into the hospital parking lot. She turned off the car and stared at the nondescript brick building in front of her. Bucks Memorial Hospital was carved into the battered cement facing over the surprisingly gleaming glass and aluminum doors.

"What am I doing here?" she whispered. Mac meant nothing to her any more. *No.* She shook her head. That wasn't true. Once he'd meant everything. She knew now that her unrealistic youthful expectations had played a part in their marriage falling apart. She breathed in until her lungs hurt and let her breath out slowly before opening the door and stepping out of the car and up the stairs to the hospital.

The heavy door resisted for a moment before opening. A sign? More likely, a reflection of her flash of cowardice. She was here. She couldn't not go in.

She found the nurses station in the intensive care unit. "Excuse me," she said.

The nurse behind the counter frowned up from the chart she'd been updating.

"Can you tell me which room Mac—Anton—Macachek is in?"

The nurse scanned her from head to toe and the frown deepened. "Only relatives are allowed to see him right now."

Concern warred with irritation. "I'm Dana Van—Dana Macachek."

"Mrs. Macachek?" the nurse asked doubtfully, going over Dana's appearance once more.

"Yes," Dana answered. She looked down at her brown linen pants and cotton sweater to see if she had put one of them on inside out or something, but saw nothing amiss. What did the woman expect, black leather? Mac was a motocross racer, not a Hell's Angel.

"What room is he in?" she asked.

"Seven Ninety. Right across the hall," the nurse answered, her attention back on the chart in front of her.

Dana turned and took another deep breath. If she didn't watch herself, soon she'd be hyperventilating. The curtains were pulled shut across the gleaming glass wall of Mac's room. Someone—the doctor?—must be with him. Otherwise, the curtains should be open so the nurse attending Mac could monitor him more easily.

Dana glanced back at the nurse working behind her, hoping Mac wasn't her patient. That wasn't fair. She didn't know the nurse or anything about her. Mac had always had that ability to make her deviate from her usual, ordered self.

Still, if Mac was hurt as critically as her morning caller had indicated, she wanted the best care for him. She made a quick silent plea for strength and crossed the hall, determined to make sure Mac was getting that care.

"Hi." A soft, pleasant voice greeted her at the doorway.

Dana looked past the still form on the bed to the nurse checking the—Mac's—monitors. Lines zigzagged and numbers flashed. She should be able to read them. Her training had taught her to. But she couldn't right now. Later.

"You're family?" the nurse asked. "Only family or close friends are allowed to visit."

Dana wondered if the nurse had added the tone of regret to her explanation in case Dana wasn't either. "I'm Dana Macachek," she assured the nurse.

"Mrs. Macachek?"

The address echoed oddly in Dana's head. It was the third time today someone had called her Mrs. Macachek, probably more times than anyone had called her that during the two-and-a-half years she and Mac had been married. Of course, how many occasions did an eighteen or nineteen-year-old girl have to be addressed as Mrs.?

"Yes," Dana finally answered.

"I'm Teresa," the short, plump woman said. "His nurse for this shift."

"How is he?"

Teresa finished checking the monitors and jotted something in Mac's chart. The pause made Dana brace herself for the worst.

"The doctor will talk with you. We'll let him know you're here."

"What can you tell me?"

"Mr. Macachek tolerated the surgery well and came to for a while in the recovery room. But he's been unconscious since."

Dana nodded, knowing that was probably all the woman was allowed to disclose.

"Would you like to sit next to him?" The nurse moved a chair over by the bed and Dana sat, hating her relief when the nurse's continuing questions drew her from having to look directly at Mac.

"Does your husband have a living will or health-care proxy?" the nurse asked.

Dana's heart skipped a beat.

"I'm sorry," Teresa said. "I didn't mean to alarm you. It's a routine question here."

"No, it's okay. He does. He did." She had no idea whether Mac still had the old proxy he'd made her agree to when they'd married. She'd fought him on it. The possibility of him being seriously hurt on the track was too real and acknowledging the fact on paper had only magnified her fears. "I have a copy at home."

"All right. I don't think we'll need it," Teresa reassured her. "I'll go let the doctor know you're here."

The walls of the room closed in on Dana with every step the nurse took toward the door. She folded her hands in her lap in a gesture of prayer, but no words formed on her lips or in her mind. Finally, she looked at Mac—really looked at *him*, not just the still form on the bed. Seven years was a long time. All she knew now of this familiar stranger was what she heard from her friend Sari Reynolds—a major motocross fan—and read in the racing magazines Dana couldn't stop herself from buying.

A few cuts and scratches on his face from the accident only emphasized the look of a fallen angel that had first drawn her to him when he'd sauntered into the youth group meeting at church all those years ago. His sole purpose had been to get her attention, get her to date him to spite her father. It had worked better than he ever could have imagined.

Her gaze moved up his face. *His hair!* It was cropped close to his head. She looked for signs of a head injury, but saw none. He'd cut his hair. As long as she had known Mac, he'd worn his hair cheek-length in front, parted in the middle. When he'd bent to kiss her, the chestnut curls had brushed her face, tickled her chin. She raised her hand to her cheek—remembering.

Mac moved, rustling the sheets and bringing Dana back to the present. He groaned and slowly opened his eyes, as if the effort might be more than he could handle. "Dana?" His cracked lips silently formed her name.

She blinked back the tears that threatened to pour down her face and took his hand in hers. "Yes, I'm here."

His eyes widened and he moistened his lips. "Your hair. You've cut your hair."

She raised her hand to her chin-length hair. It had been down to her waist when she'd left Mac. Then, the giggle started, deep inside, fed by the relief that Mac had awakened and the inanity of their both focusing on each other's hair. She tried to stop it, but she broke into laughter and tears simultaneously. The squeeze of reassurance Mac gave her hand helped her regain her control.

"Mrs. Macachek?"

There it was again. She was being Mrs.-ed to distraction. The laughter escaped again.

"Are you all right?"

Dana wiped the tears from her eyes and looked at Mac. His eyes were closed as if he'd drifted out of consciousness again. Or had she only imagined him awakening? She turned to address the person—Mac's doctor, she assumed.

"Yes, I'm fine." She rubbed her hands down the side of her slacks. "What must he think of her, breaking down like that? She rose and accepted the handshake he offered.

"I'm Dr. Sullivan."

"Dana VanAlstyne," she replied automatically.

"I'm sorry," Dr. Sullivan said, "I thought you were Mrs. Macachek." Confusion spread across his amiable face. "The nurse said she was here."

"That's me. I use my maiden name professionally. Being here at the hospital, it just popped out." She bit her tongue. *It was true*, she argued to herself. She didn't lie. In fact, Mac had once told her that she couldn't lie to save her life. Her open expression gave her away. He'd said it was one of her charms.

"You're a health-care professional?" Dr. Sullivan asked.

"A physical therapist."

Dr. Sullivan nodded. "You'll be taking him back to California, then."

"No. I mean, I don't know. My practice. I don't have a practice. I'm with the Chenango Health Network, up in New York State . . . at least for now . . . until I can open my practice." She couldn't believe she was babbling away about her job and not having her own PT practice when she was about to explode from the need to know Mac's condition.

She breathed deeply. "How bad is it?"

Dr. Sullivan frowned and looked at Mac rather than answering.

"He woke for a bit before you came in," she said.

Dr. Sullivan's eyes widened. Maybe she *had* imagined her conversation with Mac.

"Why don't you step out while I examine him? Then, we can talk in the lounge area. Ask one of the aides to get you a cup of tea or coffee or a soft drink if you want one."

Dana ran her gaze over Mac's expressionless face, fighting an urge to rub her finger across the blond stubble.

"Was there something else?" the doctor asked.

"No." The pull of the past told her to stay by Mac's side, but she made herself walk away.

~

"Okay, Mac, she's gone. You can quit pretending you're asleep."

"John?" Mac blinked his eyes for better focus.

"Yeah, I didn't know if you'd recognize me. It's been a long time."

"How could I forget after all you did for Grandma and Pops after Rudy was killed? For me, too."

He and his uncle Rudy were so close in age that they'd been more like brothers than uncle and nephew.

The doctor shrugged. "Red saved my life in Afghanistan. The little I did for your grandparents and you didn't come near to repaying him."

"How did you know . . . about me not being asleep?" he asked fending off the grief that came flowing back despite the years. Losing Rudy so soon after his dad had almost been too much for the teenaged Mac.

"Ah, the monitors don't lie. Why were you faking?"

"I wasn't sure she was real," he answered in a low voice. "Thought she might disappear if I said anything in front of you."

"Okay, then, I'll skip the lecture I should give you about toying with that young woman's feelings like that and simply tell you how lucky you are to have someone who cares as much as she does."

Mac's heart swelled at John's words. If only they were true. He thought Dana had seemed concerned, but it could be only wishful thinking. It had been so long, and at the end, she hadn't cared enough to let him in so they could grieve together.

He pushed the past from his mind. "So, Doc, what's the bad news?

Dr. Sullivan frowned.

"That bad, huh?" Mac swallowed what felt like a cotton ball lodged in his throat. He'd been kidding. He'd hoped the doctor would say he had a broken bone or two, nothing he hadn't been through before.

Dr. Sullivan sat in the chair next to the bed. "Your ankle is severely sprained, with ligament damage. You also suffered a concussion and some internal bleeding. We took care of that. But no major internal injuries."

"That doesn't sound too bad," Mac said. The doctor's manner had had him thinking much worse. "I've had broken bones and concussions before. I race motocross," he added.

"I know," Dr. Sullivan said. "My son is a fan of yours."

Mac couldn't stop the grin that spread across his face. If he lived to be one hundred, he'd never get over the wonder of people from all over the world admiring him—the bad boy of Chenango Falls.

"It's not that simple," the doctor continued. "You're going to need intensive physical therapy on that ankle just to be able to walk normally again."

"But, with therapy, I'll be fine, be able to race, right?"

"I can't promise you'll regain all the flexibility in your ankle. Someone from orthopedics will be in later to tell you more."

Dr. Sullivan's grim expression pressed Mac back into the pillow. He closed his eyes. His ankle wasn't broken. How bad could the rest be? He gathered his strength. "I was planning to retire this year anyway, while I'm still at the top. I have just one more race and I'm done."

Unadilla. Despite being the top motocross racer in the country the past three years running, he had never taken a first at Unadilla, his "hometown" track. A win there would be the grand finale of his career.

The doctor's expression didn't lighten.

"There's something else?" Mac asked.

"The CAT scan we ran because of your concussion showed a possible aneurysm in one of the blood vessels in your brain."

"So what? You want to operate?"

"Not right away. It's very small. You may have had it for years with no ill effects." Dr. Sullivan flipped through the chart. "Do you have a history of headaches, migraines?"

"Nah." Mac shook his head. "A few broken bones over the years are all."

"You've been lucky."

"I have, but I like to think part of it's skill, too."

The doctor laughed. "Skill never hurts." His expression grew more serious. "Back to your CAT scan. When you get home, have your doctor refer you to a neurologist to follow up."

"Maybe you should refer me to someone in Central New York."

"That one last race?"

"Yep."

"My advice is to think long and hard about that. Another accident, another head injury, and you could suffer a stroke. Or worse."

A picture of his grandfather after his stroke flashed in Mac's mind. He swallowed hard. But Pops had been seventy-eight. Mac was only twenty-nine. "Don't tell Dana about the aneurysm. Only about my ankle."

"As you wish," Dr. Sullivan agreed. "But you shouldn't keep it from her."

Mac bristled as he always did when someone tried to tell him what to do. He'd let Dana know about the aneurysm when and if he needed to.

Dana plopped her bag on the motel bed and surveyed the room she'd taken near the hospital. Bed, desk, dresser, TV. She pulled open the nightstand drawer. A Gideon's Bible. It was your basic economy motel room.

The nurses had given Dana Mac's few personal belongings that had been in the front seat of the SUV for safekeeping—his cell phone, a receipt from the garage where his SUV and bike had been taken, a card with his manager's name and phone number and an old cigar box that must have belonged to Mac's grandfather. Pops, as Mac had called his grandfather had been a cigar smoker. The box was taped shut, and Dana didn't pry.

While she was waiting to talk with Dr. Sullivan, Dana had called and spoken with Mac's manager, giving him the name and phone number of the garage where the vehicles were. The manager had called again when she was with the doctor. "Mike O'Brien," he'd told her voicemail. "Tell Mac I'll arrange storage for his bike until he's out of the hospital. Have him call me when he can. He totaled the Explorer, but the bike and trailer seemed to be okay. He'll want to know."

Of course, Mac would want to know. She'd always teased him about loving his bike more than he loved her. Sometimes she really thought he did.

Dana shook the memories from her head and concentrated on the present. From what Dr. Sullivan had told her, Mac's ankle was in pretty bad shape. And he had to ache all over. She'd had a minor car accident once and had been sore for days afterward.

She put her change of clothes in the dresser drawer and the few toiletries she'd brought in the bathroom. Then, she lay down for a short nap before going back to the hospital. The long drive and the tension had taken its toll. While she could hardly move or keep her eyes open, her mind raced, making sleep impossible. Professional awareness or women's intuition, she was sure there was more to Mac's condition than Dr. Sullivan had told her.

When Dana returned to the hospital, she found they'd moved Mac out of intensive care—a good sign. She maneuvered the maze of hospital wings to his new room.

Mac was up, sitting in a reclining chair watching ESPN, his leg immobile on the footrest. He grimaced as he shifted to reach the remote to turn the program off.

"Hi," she greeted him. "So you *were* awake when I was here earlier."

"Yeah."

"I thought I might have imagined it. Sore?" she asked.

"Like you wouldn't believe. How about one of those back rubs you used to give me after practice?"

Nerves she'd forgotten she had came alive at the memories of those back rubs and what they had inevitably led to. Those memories morphed into magazine and newspaper pictures of him with models, actresses and other beautiful women. Dana jerked the chair, tipping it back on two legs. It fell to the floor with a bang, and Mac raised his brows in question.

"I thought it was heavier. Guess I don't know my own strength." She sat and made the spike of jealousy subside. "I suppose I could rub the kinks out of your shoulders."

She clenched and unclenched her fingers. Where had *that* come from? Guilt?

"That would be great." He strained to sit straighter, so his shoulders weren't pressed so tightly against the vinyl back of the chair.

"Here, let me help you." She grabbed a pillow from the bed and walked to him. The hospital gown parted to show a mass of purple and blue bruising down his back. Her first instinct was to bend and kiss each ugly mark better. But then she'd never had much control where Mac was concerned. Using the pillow as a shield against touching him, she pushed him forward gently and wedged the pillow between his lower back and the chair.

He released a quiet moan.

"Sorry. I didn't mean to hurt you."

"You didn't. That was a groan in anticipation of your magic touch."

She froze, her gaze fixed on his shoulders, broad shoulders that she knew would be warm, pliant, and solid under her fingertips. *Think of him as a patient. A patient.* Her gaze moved up his clean-shaven neck, and she flexed her finger, remembering the curls that used to trail down it and how she liked to wrap them around her finger when they embraced.

"I know I'm pretty banged up," he said. "But don't be afraid to touch. I can take it."

Yeah, maybe he could, but what about her? She rested her hands on his shoulders. His muscles tensed, sending a shiver up her arm that the warmth of his skin through the thin hospital gown only intensified. To hide her reaction, she attacked his still-tense shoulders, massaging them until they softened under her fingers.

He released another low groan that nearly made her knees buckle.

"That's it," he said. "Don't stop." He closed his eyes and let his head drop back onto her hands.

His hair brushed against her skin, spiky but soft. Her fingers inched up to touch it.

"You're awfully quiet," he said.

She took a deep breath. The smell of antiseptic in the air brought her back from the dangerous place her mind was drifting to. "I, I'm—

"Excuse me." A technician pushed a cart into the room.

Dana jerked her hands from Mac and dropped them to the chair back. Heat crept up her neck, flushing her face and putting her on the defensive. *Get a grip.* They weren't two teens caught necking on the back porch by her father.

"I need to take Mr. Macachek's blood." The technician maneuvered his cart next to the chair.

She scooted away. "I'll step out of the room, so I'm out of your way."

"No need." He deftly wrapped a rubber tourniquet around Mac's bicep and rubbed his inner elbow searching for a vein. "Unless this bothers you." He looked over Mac's shoulder at her.

"No," Mac answered for her. "Dana's never been squeamish about medical stuff."

"Right," she agreed, her flight to the hall stopped by his words. Except this was Mac who was being poked and prodded, not just any patient. She could close her eyes until it was over. Instead, she focused on a small tear in the pea green vinyl of the chair back. A bit of white tufted out, begging to be stuffed back in. A condition similar to that of her emotions right now.

"One more," the technician said.

That was the second vial. How much blood did they need? And why so much? Surely, they didn't need all that to check for any infection related to his surgery. She chewed her lower lip. It didn't matter. It wasn't her business. But she couldn't help worrying about what else they might be looking for.

∽

After the technician left with a cheery "carry on," the room shouted at Mac with silence. Dana had just started to relax and warm to him when the guy had interrupted. Now, Mac would have to pitch his proposition cold.

"You're probably getting tired," Dana said.

He twisted around as much as he could.

"Do you want me to get someone to help you back into bed?"

You're not going to escape that easily. "No. Bring the other chair around. I want to talk."

Hardly daring to breathe, Mac waited for her response. This would have been so much smoother if the technician hadn't interrupted them. Of course, that had been the trademark of their relationship—someone or something interfering every time they got close.

"Talk? About the accident?" she finally asked, dragging the chair over and positioning it in front of him next to the footrest.

No, not about the accident. He tapped his good foot in impatience, but let her take the lead.

"Okay, what happened?" she asked.

"I don't know." He widened his eyes to stop the lids from drooping shut. He was tired. "I was coming around a mountain curve. I must have hit ice. Then I was here. You were here."

"About that. My being here. You still had me as the person to contact in case of an emergency. Why?"

He searched her face. Her expression was neutral. Too neutral. What did she want to hear? No, he'd better go with the truth. "It's an old card. I guess I've just transferred it from wallet to wallet over the years."

"Oh."

He looked for some sign of disappointment that he hadn't been carrying the card intentionally. Her expression didn't change.

"You should sleep." Dana voiced her dismissal in a cool, clinical tone.

But at least she'd calmly seated herself and folded her hands in her lap. He narrowed his eyes and looked harder. Little things belied her detachment. The way she scratched her pant leg with her nail. The way she wouldn't look him in the eye. He had to ask her now before she decided to leave, or he drifted off to sleep.

"You talked with Dr. Sullivan. You know I'll need physical therapy before I can get back on the circuit."

She dropped her gaze to look directly at him. Her eyes widened and her brow furled. "You can't possibly be thinking about racing. You have weeks—maybe, months—of recovery ahead."

He warmed at the note of concern. "It's those weeks of recovery I want to talk about."

"You should be talking with Dr. Sullivan, not me." She unfolded and refolded her hands in her lap.

"I did. The therapy is going to be long—and expensive. I—"

She pursed her lips the same way she always had when she disapproved of something he'd done. "Don't tell me you don't have insurance? Are you nuts? You're not twenty anymore. It's not like you're struggling to get your first break and can't afford insurance. What were you thinking?"

"Whoa." He bit back a smile. He'd almost forgotten the force of Dana in full dudgeon. "Let me finish. You might like what I have to say."

She stilled. "All right."

"I'm not twenty anymore," he started.

The corner of her mouth quirked up.

"I have insurance. I can handle the cost."

She nodded.

"I just want to get out of here as soon as I can, and the docs will want to have my treatment set up first."

"So . . . what? You want me to help you arrange to get back to California and start therapy? The hospital social worker will handle all that."

"I'm not going back to California. Not right away. I'm not sure the doctors would let me. And I don't want to start PT here and then have to switch to a different therapist at home."

"Oh. I guess I assumed you'd go back home, I hadn't considered that you might not be able to right away."

"My bike's here. I won't be racing the rest of the schedule—except Unadilla. Might as well stay East."

"You *are* nuts. In your condition, how can you even be thinking about racing at Unadilla? It's too soon. Way too soon."

He bristled. "I know what I'm doing. The doctors said with work I can be ready."

She shook her head. "You aren't planning to stay at the farm are you?"

So, she knew he'd kept his grandparents' place.

"When was the last time you were out there?" she asked. "No one's lived there for what, eight years? The windows are all smashed and the porch roof collapsed during a snow storm last winter."

He smiled to himself. Not only did she know he'd kept the farm, but she checked up on it. A wave of nostalgia flowed through him. They'd spent a lot of time there, since he hadn't been welcome at her family's home. Made some good memories.

"No, not the farm." He paused. "I thought I'd stay with you."

PREQUEL TO
SWEET ENTANGLEMENT

Meet a younger Jesse and Lauren in *A Team Macachek Christmas*, a Team Macachek novella. An excerpt follows.

EXCERPT FROM
A TEAM MACACHEK
CHRISTMAS

CHAPTER 1

"I definitely plan on going to the Christmas party." *That voice. It had haunted him since summer.* Jesse Brewster pushed himself up to a sitting position on the lounge couch and muted the sound of the race video he was studying on the ninety-inch TV.

It couldn't be. He shook his head to block the sound, dispel the memories and ran his hand through his disheveled hair. Lauren was at Syracuse University taking finals.

"See you," Royce Evans, one of the other Team Macachek racers said distinctly.

"Right." Her voice again.

Or Syracuse was the place Lauren was *supposed* to be. Her and Royce? Jesse worked a muscle in his jaw. Was that the real reason she'd stopped coming to his races, sent him the break-up text? Jesse unmuted the TV and jacked up the sound to drown out his thoughts and anything else he might hear from the hall.

He placed his elbows on his knees and focused on the action. To perfect his technique, he studied videos of his motocross races, wins and losses, to see what he had done right and wrong and what his competitors had done right. It was his job and ambition to be the best. Jesse frowned at his less-than-stellar execution of a jump. By his account, he had to rack up enough winnings in the next ten years or so to invest for the rest of his life. Given his lack of success with the online engineer degree at Arizona State University his parents and Lauren had pressured him into, what else could he do that was anywhere near as lucrative as racing? Limit pressuring him to his parents. Period. Where Lauren was concerned, it had been his need to impress her by proving he could do more than race, be more for her.

"Oh, I didn't know anyone was in here."

Jesse swung his head around and froze at the virtual sucker punch that slugged him in the gut. It hadn't been his imagination. Lauren Cooper stood in the doorway in all her blond glory. His imagination never gave justice to the real thing.

"Jesse?" Her voice was barely above a whisper but loud enough to send a shiver through him.

His muscles tensed. *I can do this.* Jesse rose and faced the one and only woman he had ever loved. "I'm as surprised to see you as you are to see me. I figured it would be finals week, that you'd still be in Syracuse."

He didn't ask what she was doing here in the barracks, as the guys on the team called the resort-like facility Mac Macachek, the owner of the racing team, had built at the team's headquarters in Chenango Falls—Mac's hometown in Central New York. After hearing her with Royce in the hall, Jesse didn't want to know.

"I uh, had early finals." Lauren stared at her feet.

What was that about? Unless she regretted what she'd done to him. His heart raced *Yeah, right.* He was one sick puppy when it came to Lauren Cooper. He should have seen the writing on the wall when he'd told her last June that he'd only signed up for one class at the University of Arizona Online for the fall semester. He'd barely made Cs in everything but his one engineering class in the spring semester. After that, she'd started coming up with excuses for not coming to his races, even when he'd offered to pay for her travel and, then boom, *The Text.*

"You're here for the team Christmas party?" she asked

"Didn't your Aunt Sari tell you?"

Confusion spread across Lauren's perfect face. "Tell me what?"

"I hadn't intended to come, but she made me co-chair-whatever of the party planning after the fire at The Manor wiped out the plans to have the party there. Went and told Mac that." Lauren's aunt had been a huge fan of Mac's. When he'd retired, she'd transferred her allegiance to Jesse, even coming to some of the races Lauren had said she couldn't make. "I couldn't let Mac down. I had to come."

Lauren laughed, but the sound lacked the bouncy spontaneity he was used to.

"Yes, I know how Sari is." Lauren scuffed her foot on the floor, and Jesse dropped his gaze from her face. She gripped the handle of a vacuum in one hand, the pail of cleaning supplies in the other.

"I'll come back later when you're finished in here," she said.

He nodded at the cleaning supplies, not ready to let her go, pathetic case that he was. "So, like, you're working for Mac during the semester break."

"Something like that." She wouldn't meet his gaze.

"You can do your thing. I'm just watching the video from High Point, the competition Sari drove down to Pennsylvania for with *just* Mac and Dana." Yeah, he was getting in a dig. That was the first race Lauren had cancelled out on.

"I was beat, just coming off final exams."

As if anything to do with school had ever been a problem for Lauren. He had to get this over with. He strode to her, took the vacuum from her hand, and took her hand in his. "We need to talk. You wouldn't take any of my calls. I gave you your space for the summer like you said you wanted." Jesse searched her eyes and thought he saw something there of the love and desire they'd shared for almost two years. Of course, he could be seeing what he wanted to see.

"Then, boom, in September, I get an *it's not working* text."

Lauren pulled her hand from his, sending a chill up his arm. "It wasn't working. The distance. Us, our lives, we're too different. We, I…" She stumbled over her words.

He wanted to shout *BS*. Aside from his racing, Lauren was the only thing that had worked in his life for a long while.

She straightened. "Besides, from the guys, sounds like you're doing okay, uh, socially."

The guys? Royce? Royce was on the road a lot, too, except he'd stayed here in the northeast for arenacross for the winter, while Jesse had gone back to his native California outdoor tracks to race.

He folded his arms across his chest. "If you mean the pit tootsies, they don't mean anything. And, I'm sure what you've heard is an exaggeration." Especially, if Royce, or whoever was Lauren's source of information, thought he had a chance with her.

"No, it's not that." Her voice and expression were devoid of any emotion.

He stopped himself from pulling her into his arms and kissing the fake—it had to be fake—indifference out of her. "Then, what is it?"

She released a pent-up breath. "We can't be anything more than friends, nothing more than what I am to the other team members. That's it."

So, she and Royce weren't a thing?

Lauren grabbed the vacuum. "I've got to get to my other work." Her blond braid swinging with her forceful steps, she made her getaway without even a goodbye.

Jesse stared at the closed door. That wasn't all. Not by a long shot. In the couple of weeks left before his flight back to California, he'd find the real reason for Lauren's behavior. He refused to believe she didn't love him anymore.

Lauren leaned against the door, feeling Jesse's gaze drilling into her from the other side. His pull. Her feelings. They were still there. She couldn't, wouldn't let him distract her again. Having him as a part of her life was like wearing blinders. She only saw the shadows of anything else going on. And look where that had gotten her and her mother. She'd had no inkling her father… Lauren shook her thoughts from her head.

"Are you okay?"

Lauren opened her eyes at Dana Macachek's question.

"'Ren, 'kay?" Dana and Mac's two-year-old, Rudy, toddled over and patted Lauren's leg.

"I'm okay, sweetie." Lauren ruffled his baby blond hair. "You knew Jesse was here?"

"Ah, that's what the look is about."

Lauren shrugged her tense shoulders. "He surprised me when I went to clean the lounge."

"I didn't know he was coming. Neither did Mac until Jesse signed in the computer register when he arrived last night."

"He said Aunt Sari asked him to help her with the new arrangements for the team Christmas party."

Dana reached down and scooped up Rudy who was headed back in the direction they'd come from. "No, you don't, partner."

"Daddy. Bikes," he said.

"We'll see the bikes after I finish talking with Lauren."

"'Ren, bikes?" Rudy asked.

"Sorry, pal. I have to finish my work," Lauren answered, thankful that the conversation had moved away from Jesse.

"Work, bikes."

Lauren laughed. Rudy was adorable. When he was born, Jesse had still been living with Dana and Mac at the house. The barracks hadn't been built. She'd shared her surprise at Jesse's ease with the newborn. He'd grinned the smile she'd thought of as her smile and said, "What can I say. I'm a kid magnet." They'd talked about kids and, since they were both only children, agreed three sounded right. It seemed like a lifetime ago.

She swallowed the lump in her throat. "That's not my job." Lauren pushed the vacuum forward.

"Vroom," he said.

"Maybe it's the noise," Dana said. "In addition to motorcycles, he's a fan of vacuuming, the electric mixer, and the juicer." Dana's expression grew serious. "You are okay? Seeing Jesse? It's probably none of my business, but if you need to talk sometime, I've been there."

"I'm all right, really. Jesse and I are friends." Although Jesse's parting look had been anything but friendly. "And not to be rude, but I need to finish so I can pick Mom up from work. Her car's in the shop."

"Sure, but my offer stands. Come on, Rudy. Let's go fix bikes with Daddy."

"Daddy. Bikes." He shot down the hall with Dana fast on his heels.

Lauren wished she could talk with Dana. But her problems were her own to solve. The past six months since her father had left, dealing with her mother's helplessness, had taught Lauren that she needed to be strong and self-sufficient. She placed the cleaning bucket on the floor outside the lounge and attacked sweeping the hall carpet with a vengeance. Dana and Mac's situation had been similar, but different. They'd been married at Lauren and Jesse's age, although soon after, they'd been torn apart by Dana's father and the distrust he created. Mac and Dana hadn't gotten together again for seven years.

Other problems aside, Dana had never been in the financial bind concerning college that Lauren was in. She couldn't take another semester off her studies at Syracuse or she could lose her full tuition scholarship. Her elbow cracked with the force of her effort. She *had* to get the grant she'd applied for. Her father had decided to renege on his promise to pay for that part of her education, and her mother was in too much denial over her situation to pursue any separation or support agreement. Even working full-time, what she'd put away from taking the fall semester off and working didn't come close to covering all of her room and board. Not after the financial help she'd had to give her mother. Lauren pushed her hair behind her ear. Jesse had tried to be there for her—too much. She wasn't about to become dependent on a man like her mother had.

When Lauren hit the far end of the hall, she sensed as much as heard the door to the lounge open and shut and crossed her fingers that Jesse's room or wherever he was headed was in the opposite direction. Breath held, she turned and caught Jesse disappearing through the doorway to the second floor and hurried back to the lounge. She glanced at the computer printout tucked in the cleaning bucket. Jesse must have gotten in really late yesterday or early this morning. No second-floor rooms were on her cleaning list for today. Her stomach dropped. But his room, filled with his things, his presence, would be on her list tomorrow.

She pushed opened the lounge door. Jesse's cologne, his distinct sea and wind scent clogged her throat with a longing she'd thought she'd finally locked away. She ground her teeth. She didn't need Jesse Brewster. She didn't need anyone but herself.

Made in the USA
Middletown, DE
30 May 2023